The Specters of Algeria

HWANG YEO JUNG

Translated by Yewon Jung

Honford
Star

This translation first published by Honford Star 2023

Honford Star Ltd.
Profolk, Bank Chambers
Stockport
SK1 1AR
honfordstar.com

알제리의 유령들 © 2017 황여정
THE SPECTERS OF ALGERIA © 2017 Hwang Yeo Jung
Translation copyright © 2023 Yewon Jung
All rights reserved
Original Korean edition published by Munhakdongne Publishing Corp.
English translation rights arranged with Munhakdongne Publishing Corp.
The moral rights of the translators and editors have been asserted.

ISBN (paperback): 978-1-7398225-6-9
ISBN (ebook): 978-1-7398225-7-6
A catalogue record for this book is available from the British Library.

Printed and bound by TJ Books
Cover design by Jaemin Lee
Typeset by Honford Star

This book is published with the support of the
Literature Translation Institute of Korea (LTI Korea).

1 3 5 7 9 10 8 6 4 2

Contents

Part One

YUL'S STORY

1

It was probably late summer.

Or maybe it was late spring. It wasn't late autumn or winter, that I know.

No, I *don't* know. I remember only two things for sure: the languorous heat and the feeling that a season was nearing its end. It could have been the room that was so hot, not the season; it could have been a certain period of time, not a season, that was nearing its end.

At any rate, we were talking that day about how the mold that had been spreading out of control on the ceiling and onto a wall had somehow disappeared. To be precise, we were talking about how sad we were that the mold had disappeared, and to be even more precise, we were thinking about a conversation we'd had when the mold had been expanding its territory.

I think it was that summer, or the summer before that—I can't be certain—but anyway, the rainy season was unusually drawn out, that summer of the growing mold. The heavy rain that pelted down day after day crushed the flowerbed my dad had so carefully tended to, and weeds grew thick and strong, spreading throughout the yard. Humidity seeped into the corners of the ceiling and the walls and wouldn't lift even after days had passed, and then came the mold. I had never seen mold in the house before. I said it scared me, and Jing said it was just mold. I didn't care if it was just mold, or whatever else it was. The spreading grayish-black spot seemed to portend that something was rotting, and the thought of rotting things led to thoughts of other dreadful things. Vermin and corpses, for instance. I voiced my thought, and Jing was quiet for a while. He did that sometimes. His mouth shut tight, he would let his gaze wander and become lost in thought. And slowly knit his brows. I found him charming when he did this, though I couldn't tell what he was thinking. He always smiled as he came out of his silence, his eyes on me. Smiling and looking at me as always, he said, "Mold isn't just mold, you know."

"What is it, then?" I asked.

"It's the earth."

"What do you mean, the earth?"

"Take a good look," Jing said, pointing to the part of the mold covering up a corner of the ceiling.

"Doesn't it remind you of something?" he asked.

"Like what?"

"Iceland."

"Huh?"

"It looks exactly like Iceland."

"What on earth are you talking about?"

"On a world map, I mean."

I couldn't recall. I tilted my head and Jing said, "Bring me your student atlas."

The Specters of Algeria

"It's not here."

"Did you leave it at school?"

"No."

"Well?"

I hesitated for a moment and said, "He burned it. There isn't a single book left in this house now. You know that."

"Even your textbooks?"

"They *are* books."

Jing fell silent. He let his gaze wander and became lost in thought. Then he smiled and asked me to bring him some paper and a pencil.

He drew a world map in a single stroke. I didn't have an atlas or a knack for geography, so I couldn't tell how precise Jing's map was, but it seemed exactly like a world map, as I remembered it, at least. The contours of the continents, with their fine, distinct curves, the confusing boundary lines on the inside, and more than forty country names all served to raise his credibility. Above all, the effortless movements of his hand, as well as the confidence in his eyes, told me that it was the real thing. I would have trusted his map, in fact, even if it were completely different from the real one. Jing's map was Jing's, and anything that was Jing's was absolutely right. I was stunned, though, because even though I believed he was absolutely right in everything, I didn't think that he would be *good* at everything.

"What, are you a genius now?" I said.

"It could just be that you're an idiot" was Jing's reply.

He put his index finger on a spot on the map and said, "This is Iceland. Now compare the two carefully."

I looked from Jing's Iceland to the mold's Iceland. I couldn't say that they were exactly the same, but they almost were.

"Now take a look at the others," Jing said, and with him as my guide, I discovered many countries camouflaged as mold. The mold continued to spread day by day, and I discovered more and more countries. Some countries had complicated names I could hardly pronounce. We started out by wondering how they had come to have such names and ended up wondering who had named the countries and when, if a country needed a name, if there was a country without a name, what you should call a nameless country, if you could call it a country when you couldn't call it by any name at all, and so on and so forth. The more we talked, the less afraid I became of the mold.

As soon as the rainy season came to an end, my dad tore off all the wallpaper in the house and painted the walls. It wasn't because of the mold. Or maybe it was. If it wasn't for the mold, he wouldn't have paid attention to something like wallpaper, and wouldn't even have realized that the walls had been papered in the first place.

My dad was afraid of paper. At first he was afraid of books, then he was afraid of paper with words written on them; in the end, he grew afraid of paper itself.

Before the rainy season began—on a day that was just before the rainy season, or much before, I can't say—he up and left home; then he returned one day out of nowhere. I don't remember how long he'd been gone. It was quite long—I'd waited and waited and waited, and then waited some more—but I'm not sure if *long* was the time I spent waiting, or the feeling I had in my heart. Or were they the same? At any rate, it was the first time that he'd done something like that. When he came home, he just lay curled up in his room, looking sapped; then one day, he took down all the books from the shelves and piled them up in the yard, then poured kerosene on them and set them on fire. All my storybooks, textbooks, reference books; workbooks were thrown into the fire as well. He trembled all over, watching the raging fire. I burst into tears. *Dad, what's the matter?* I said over and over, and he finally turned around to look at me. *Books frighten me,* he said. *You're frightening me!* I wanted to say, but the words were buried in my sobs.

All the paper in the house was gone; the wallpaper was the last to go. Only after the wallpaper had been burned and the walls painted did I realize that even the box containing Jing's letters was gone. Jing had fashioned the box out of blue hardboard, and more importantly, the box had held his map. I'd kept the box hidden in a corner above the kitchen cabinet. There was no telling when and how my dad had discovered it.

I chose crying over demanding to know why he'd done it. He gently patted my head. "Don't worry, your mom will be home soon, too," he said irrelevantly, which made me sob even harder. "Do you want to go to the zoo?" he asked. "You love the zoo. The animals at Changgyeong Park have all moved to Seoul Grand Park, I hear. They say it's much bigger and better than the old park, with a lot more animals, too." I went on crying.

Jing said that he could draw me any number of world maps. When he said that, I felt somehow that the letters were an even greater loss. He said that he'd write me more letters than he ever had before.

"But what about the mold?" I asked.

"What about it?" Jing asked in return.

"My dad sprayed mold cleaner on it. And that paint, it's not just any paint. It's mold proof. It doesn't matter how much of a genius you are—you can't bring mold back to life."

Some time passed, and one day late that summer, or late spring the next year, or maybe even late autumn or winter—which would surprise me—we calmly reflected on the process in which the mold had formed and led to the burning of the map. Then we stopped talking. We stared and stared at the wall with a faraway gaze, like old people longing for their prime which exists only in their minds. The wall looked fresh and clean, as if nothing had happened, and I got goosebumps for some reason. I said so and Jing nodded, saying, "That's entirely possible."

I nodded in reply, though I couldn't tell whether he was referring to the wall or the goosebumps, and whether he was saying it was a good thing or bad.

I went to the front door to see him out but stopped by the bathroom before he left. I had opened the door and was about to come out when I heard my dad's voice.

"I slept with your mom" were the words.

I froze, my hand on the doorknob.

He repeated the words, enunciating them slowly and clearly as if speaking to someone hard of hearing.

"I, slept, with, your, mom."

Jing stood at the door with his shoes on, looking up at my

dad, who was standing in the living room with his back to me, looking down at him. The bathroom faced the front door, slightly at an angle, so I could see Jing's face, but I don't remember the look on that face.

Jing's eyes turned to me. Only then did my dad realize that I was there and turned his head a little to the right, then stopped and turned it to the left; then he turned around and went into his room.

I don't remember how long Jing and I stayed standing there like that, either.

Jing raised his arm and urged me to come to him. I opened the bathroom door all the way and did as he asked, and put my shoes on. He took my hand in his as we went out the door.

At the gate, Jing kissed me. It was my first time, but I wasn't flustered. His lips felt cold and rough. Jing had to lower his head even though I was standing a step above him, and I was a little surprised, after our lips separated, to realize how tall he was. I had been taller than him at one time.

"When did you get so tall?" I asked.

Jing grinned, placed my right hand on his left palm, then looked down at my hand for a long time.

"It'll be all right," he said.

"What will?"

"Everything. Everyone."

He stood at the end of the alley, waving and smiling more brightly than ever, then disappeared out of view. I stood at the gate longer than usual. Then I darted off into the alley and turned the corner. He was gone.

Two years passed before I saw him again.

It was the first day of my mom's funeral. The funeral was held at home, as my dad wished. His theater colleagues arranged and oversaw all the proceedings.

Jing and his mom bowed to my mom's portrait, and then we stood face to face. We bowed to each other, and Jing's mom took my dad's hands in hers. He dropped his head on her shoulder and wept.

Jing and I stood looking at each other without a word. I'd grown quite tall, but so had he.

My dad calmed down, and Jing and his mom left.

Three years later, I saw him again. It was at his dad's funeral. Jing alone greeted my dad and me. After the mutual bow, my dad asked, "Where's your mom?"

"She passed out … We put her on an IV," he said.

His voice was thick and low. It sounded unfamiliar, but it suited him.

My dad squeezed his arm lightly, then let go.

Jing passed in front of me three times while my dad had a bottle of soju. Once, he glanced at me. He stopped for a brief moment and smiled at me. I wanted to smile back, but couldn't.

My dad and I left the funeral hall without seeing his mom.

Jing and I were twenty, and that was the last we saw of each other.

The Specters of Algeria

*

I imagined running into Jing. There he would be—on a subway, on a bus, in a bookstore, in a café, on the street—when I casually turned my steps or my head. What we would talk about, what we would do, where we would go, I couldn't say; and the scene—or the scenes—would always stop at us running into each other, because I couldn't really imagine what would happen next.

And—

I also imagined that I would never see him again. Jing was running as far as he could. He would run so far that even if he wanted to return, his life would come to an end before he could; and in the hour—or the hours—searching for one another we wouldn't find even a trace of each other, not anywhere.

And—

Days went by as I didn't imagine anything.

2

I didn't go to college. I couldn't. My head ached whenever I read a book for more than three minutes—whether it was a textbook or a workbook, or whatever it was. I don't remember when that started happening. After my dad burned all the books, there was nothing to read at home; at school, I would sit staring off into space all day. I was made aware of my symptoms by my homeroom teacher in my second year of high school. After I submitted my answer sheet for the monthly exam with the same numbers marked over and over for three months in a row, he had my dad come see him.

"She won't make it to college at this rate," he said.

"It's up to her," my dad said—according to himself.

My teacher remembered differently.

"You need to take more interest in your daughter," he had said.

"I'm not interested" was my dad's reply.

My homeroom teacher asked me if he was my biological father. I said yes, and he looked at me with great sympathy.

Every Saturday afternoon, my teacher held a make-up class for me and five other kids. I still just stared at the desk or the blackboard, textbook or workbook, at my teacher's face or his finger holding a chalk, or just off into space. He tried various methods in an attempt to get us to focus but gave up in the end and just had us read the textbook out loud. Before I made it to the end of the second page, I had to grasp my head with my hands because of the ringing in my ears and a splitting headache. My teacher said that he wanted to see my dad again. He was away on a trip, though.

"On a trip where?" my teacher asked.

"He was in Gangwon-do three days ago. I don't know where he is now," I said.

"What is this world coming to?" he mumbled to himself, then declared:

"Your life is yours! You can live the life you want if you set your mind to it!"

A life of reading nothing, that was what I wanted.

"Do you understand?" he asked.

"Yes," I said, nodding my head, meaning that I'd made up my mind to quit school and live the life I wanted, as he'd suggested.

"Will you go to college?" he asked.

I was thrown off guard.

"Or will you give up?"

I kept silent, not knowing what he wanted me to do.

"What matters is your own will. Your own will!"

My silence stretched on.

"Let me know when you've made up your mind. I'll be waiting."

I told my dad about the exchange after he returned from his trip.

The Specters of Algeria

"My teacher's a little nuts," I said.

He nodded slowly and said, "Yes, he does seem a bit inconsistent. But ..."

"But what?"

"That was a nice thing he said."

"What was?"

"That he'll be waiting."

I gave him a blank stare and said, "What is this? Were you secretly hoping that I'd go to college, too?"

He gave me a blank stare in return and said, "I mean, I like how he said he'll be waiting. Waiting, waiting for something, you know."

Something dropped with a soft thud in my heart. It wasn't heavy. It felt as if it had gently landed somewhere.

*

We moved in the autumn of the year Jing's dad died. My dad's theater colleagues helped with the move. After everything had been loaded onto the truck, my dad took a careful look around the house. I did the same, feeling somehow that I should. The house had been handed down to my dad from my grandfather. My dad had been born and raised in the house. So had I, and my mom had come to live in the house after they got married, and she died there. Could you say that we were connected through the house? I suppose. But I'll never know how they each had spent their days there. And they would never know everything about the days I had spent there. Only the house had been witness to all the moments we'd lived through inside. I stared at each and every corner of the house more deliberately than did my dad, as if I were searching for something, anything. The house remained empty and silent. It was just a house, after all.

The new house had an unusual structure. We rented the half-basement floor of a two-story building standing on the edge of a slope; seen from the bottom of the hill, where we lived was on the ground floor, and the building appeared to have three stories. In other words, half of the house was underground, and the other half above the ground. Inside, the house was in the form of a long, horizontal trapezoid. In the space aboveground was a corridor that served as a veranda, and there were also a kitchen and a bathroom; in the space below were two small rooms, a large room, and a living room. I used the large room, and my dad, one of the small rooms. The other small room was full of stuff such as a refrigerator and a vacuum cleaner, and the living room was furnished with a low sofa and table, and a television. The large room was bigger than the living room, so it looked empty even with a wardrobe, a bed, and a dressing table; I said I would use the small room, but my dad wouldn't allow it, saying the large room had a window facing the corridor where some light came through, but the small room had no windows and was always dark. I insisted that I could go outside for some sun, but he wouldn't hear of it.

"When you're awake you can be in a room a hundred floors underground, but when you're sleeping, you need to be somewhere the sun has touched."

"But what about you?"

The Specters of Algeria

"I've slept in a place like that for fifty years."

"So?"

"So I have plenty of sun already in me."

"Twenty years is a long time, too."

"Yes, it's a long time."

"Well?"

"Well, it's long but not nearly long enough."

"Why not?"

"Because, that's the way of the sun."

"What's that supposed to mean?"

"If you don't know, just be quiet and listen to your dad."

I thought the room would go on feeling empty and dreary, but to my surprise, I got used to it in just one month. I slept an average of eight hours every day without waking once during the night.

Before the move, I always woke up a couple of times while sleeping, sometimes for no reason, and sometimes from a nightmare. The nightmares were varied: the entire house would be on fire, burning furiously; my mom would be staring at me, while standing upside down; people in uniforms would march in step toward me, their pace growing faster and faster; or the world would be covered by glaciers everywhere. Sometimes I had trouble falling asleep for fear that I would have another nightmare. In those moments, I sat up and called out, *Jing! Jing! Jing!* He made no reply, but I felt relieved just calling out to him.

I slept longer and longer. Once, I slept through the entire day, plus a quarter of the next; when I woke up, my dad was sitting in the middle of the room, with a meal prepared on a portable dining table. I started, then climbed hesitantly down from my bed and sat across from him. He put a spoon in my hand.

"I'm not hungry," I said.

"Just have a little bite," he said.

My hand, holding the spoon, dropped to the table. He took the spoon from me, scooped up some steamed rice, and held it before my mouth. I resisted for a while, but opened my mouth in the end. As I slowly chewed the rice, my mouth watered and I felt a pang of hunger. Only then did I notice the side dishes. There was beef radish soup, salt-dried corvina, steamed eggs, seasoned bean sprouts, seasoned spinach, salted pollack roe, and cubed radish kimchi—all things I loved. I gobbled up my bowl of rice. Then I grew drowsy again.

"Will you try and do something?" my dad asked.

"Do what?"

"Anything."

I slipped back into bed. He said something more, but I drifted off to sleep.

When I opened my eyes, he was still sitting there. After some dawdling, I went and again, sat across from him.

"What do I have to do?" I asked.

"What you want to do."

"Like what?"

"Whatever you want."

"Whatever?"

"Whatever."

From the look of him, he wouldn't stir, it seemed, unless I said something. If I didn't, I would have trouble sleeping again. Once I decided to give it some thought, though, something did come to mind: an image of him sitting in front of a sewing machine, and my mom sewing. He was making costumes for the theater actors, and she was working on a quilt, or mending our clothes or bags. The scene was familiar to me, something I had often seen since I was a child.

"Mending," I said.

"What do you mean, mending?" my dad asked.

"Mending clothes, I mean."

"You're saying you want to mend clothes?"

"Yeah."

"It's not as easy as it seems."

"You said I could do whatever I wanted."

"You really want to try it?"

"Yeah."

He left the room at last, and I crawled back under the blanket.

When I woke up again, he led me out to the living room without a word, and showed me a desk-type sewing machine, saying that he had found it at a market in Jongno. It was secondhand but cost quite a bit, he said with pride. I stared at it, puzzled.

"You said you wanted to mend clothes," he said.

"Oh," I said.

"Here, have a seat."

Feeling awkward, I sat down; to my surprise, though, I felt comfortable, both in body and mind. I sat still for a moment, then gently stroked the desk and the machine. The dry, smooth surface felt familiar to the touch.

"Yes, you always wipe the worktable clean before you get down to work. Preferably with a dry towel, not your hand," my dad said, giving me my first lesson in sewing.

Sewing, I quickly mastered. In a sort of introductory phase, I made dresses, pants, shirts, and jackets, over and over in different sizes, which wasn't as difficult as I'd expected. Of course, I didn't make an attempt at designing clothes; I just learned the basics of cutting and sewing. At any rate, the process in which something was created from nothing through my own hands amazed me every time.

The problem was mending. It was considerably harder than what my dad had said in warning.

He would bring me cheap clothes from the market and hand me a piece of clothing along with a drawing of a different person each time, leaving it to me to make necessary adjustments. Included in each drawing were the height, weight, and age of the person.

"I really love this dress, but the shoulder and waistlines are too old-fashioned. The fabric is nice, and the color and pattern are pretty, so I think it'll look as good as new with a bit of adjustment," my dad would say, placing the "order," and I would have to make adjustments accordingly, as the person in the drawing wished. In my opinion the color and pattern were all wrong to begin with, and the problem lay in the customer's figure, not the lines of the clothing, but such arguments weren't allowed. I was only permitted to ask in more detail about what the customer had in mind. The orders became more difficult with time, and I had to ask more and more questions. At times he made preposterous demands, and at times, he repeated the same thing he'd said in the beginning; and then there were times when he said he'd come back. When nothing seemed to work, even when I did as I'd learned, I became exasperated.

"What do you want me to do?" I snapped.

"Do you think you can do it if I tell you what I want?"

"Well, what is it that you want?"

"Is that what you're going to say to a customer?"

"So what do you want from me?"

"How am I supposed to know?"

"If the customer doesn't know, who does?"

"I'm not a customer. I'm your dad."

I snatched the piece of clothing from the sewing machine and hurled it to the floor, leaping to my feet. I went into my room and slammed the door shut. I lay in bed fuming. *He's awful. He's just awful,* I thought.

I don't know how long I stayed that way. Toward the evening, he tapped on my door. I stayed in bed without answering.

"Yul," he called out.

I flipped over to the other side.

"Yul," he called out again.

I sat up and shouted, "What! What! What do you want from me?"

He opened the door carefully and said in a low voice, "It's time for dinner."

I fumed some more, then calmed myself and went out to the living room and ate.

We had more of these fights, but the more we fought, the less angry I became. In the end, I was almost unperturbed.

Sometimes I stopped asking questions, and sometimes I redirected the questions. If I didn't get a clear answer, I made adjustments in the clothing without the answer. I felt that if the customer changed his mind because we couldn't get through to each other, there wasn't much that I could do. When things reached that point, he would say in a very low voice, as if to tell me a big secret, that the important thing was to focus on what the customer had requested in the beginning. That's where everything lay; to believe that was the key.

"What do you mean by that?" I once asked.

"You must believe that the person knows more about the piece of clothing than anyone else, that it's the customer, not you, who has thought the most about the changes that should be made, and because of that, everything was expressed in the initial request they made. First, you must believe that. Only then can you understand that there's no contradiction or ambiguity in their demand. That's what it means to get to someone's mind, and that's the only way to find out how the piece of clothing should turn out. Questions are necessary only to reconfirm the wishes of the person whose mind you have reached."

I couldn't quite grasp what he was saying, but the words sobered me, and I couldn't say anything back.

Later on, whenever I recalled the words, I shook my head. You can always make adjustments to satisfy customers by checking a few details, but you can never get to someone's mind, no matter how strongly you believe in something. The words sounded plausible on the surface, but had nothing to do with reality, I concluded. I wanted to ask my dad if he had

The Specters of Algeria

flat out lied to me, or if he really hadn't known; but he was dead by then and there was no way for me to find out.

*

He died of acute indigestion. He was staying at a bed and breakfast in Daepyeong-ri, Jeju-do. The owner knocked on his door because my dad didn't come out of his room long past noon, then went inside because there was no answer, only to find him collapsed on the floor with a big half-eaten dumpling in his hand.

A dumpling.

My dad didn't like dumplings. He didn't like flour, first of all, and he didn't like foods cooked with mashed-up ingredients, such as potato salad and seafood pancakes. They were sticky, he said, and didn't have much to chew on. My mom was the one who liked dumplings. She liked making dumplings, to be exact. She said she felt peaceful and reverent when she was making dumplings.

It was November, and my dad had been away on a trip for two months.

After my mom died, he took frequent trips. He would be gone for anywhere from three days to two months. There was no telling when he would leave or come back. He would go off after a walk around the neighborhood, after having dinner with someone, or while out shopping. He would call me on the first day to let me know that he was leaving, then come back or call me again on the third day; the three days would turn into five, then a week, then two weeks, and then a month. After he began to teach me how to mend clothes, he normally went away for no longer than three days at a time, for a week at most; but after the lessons came to an end, the trips became long again. The calls were brief. I would ask him where he was, and he would tell me.

A month before he died, he'd said that he was in Wan-do.

"Is that an island?" I asked.

"Yeah," he replied.

"Did you take a boat?"

"No."

"How did you get there, then?"

"I took a bus."

"But you said it's an island."

"There's a road that leads to it."

"Yeah?"

"Don't you know these things?"

"Well, it's not really an island, then, is it?"

"It's not?"

"It's not."

"You're doing all right, aren't you?"

"Yeah. What about you, Dad?"

"I'm all right."

That was our last conversation.

I took mending classes for a year and a half, then opened an alteration shop six months later. The shop was in a cheaply rented space of about thirteen square feet, in a corner of the first floor of the building in which we lived. It had been used as a kitchen by the owner of a bakery across the street, but the bakery closed down from lack of business. Several months passed, but no one wanted the place because of the inadequate space, so my dad seized the opportunity. For the opening ceremony party, he invited his theater colleagues. One of them brought a pig's head for good luck; another brought a prayer he'd written, wishing me great success; and another brought a handmade sign for the shop. The sign read, "Yul Alterations." Yul was my birth name. Even after I became Eunjo, they all called me Yul. I called them Uncle or Aunt So-and-so. Someone pointed out that he should have made clear on the sign what items could be altered, and someone else added that people might think I altered all sorts of things. For the first time in years things were lively at home, and I laughed again and again.

Late that night, when about half the people had gone home, and about half the remaining people had fallen asleep, some-one said, "It's about time you came back, don't you think?"

It was Uncle Osu. I was dozing off, my head against the armrest of the living room sofa.

"If you don't want to direct, you can be the dramaturg," he said.

After a long pause my dad said, "Yeah, it's about time."

On the third anniversary of his death, I went to Jeju. I hadn't really meant to go for the anniversary. I woke up earlier than usual that day, and it was snowing. It was the first snow of the year, a bit early. The sky was clear and the wind gentle, and the soft snow fell and piled up nicely. I opened the win-dow and reached out a hand, letting the snow fall on my palm. I took a look, and the edges of the flakes were sharper than

I'd imagined, like shards of glass. The edges quickly melted away, and the moisture soon vanished into the air; or should I say, returned?

I looked out the window again. The snow looked strange somehow, as though I had never seen snow falling before. Maybe it really was my first time, watching the snow to see how it fell.

I left to go to work and saw someone's footprints in the alley. They were quite large, but neat and straight, as if the person had taken each step with care. I didn't want to mess them up, so I came out of the alley, carefully walking next to the footprints. The footprints went past the shop to the main street, and without really thinking about it, I followed them and went on walking. As I walked, something told me that I should go to Jeju.

I had never been to Jeju before. I thought it was quite far away, but once I got there, I realized I could make two trips there and back in a day if I wanted to.

I spent a week at the bed and breakfast where my dad had stayed. There was nothing to do except eat, sleep, walk, and sit. I wanted some dumplings, but I didn't see a dumpling shop. I asked the owner of the bed and breakfast and was told that there was a Chinese restaurant three bus stops away.

"Do they have king-sized dumplings?" I asked.

"I don't know, but they do have fried dumplings," the owner said.

On my last day there, I ran into her on the beach. Even from a distance, I recognized her at once. She didn't recognize me, though, even when she came near.

3

After my first and last trip to Jeju, I didn't close the shop for ten years, not even for a day. My work hours weren't fixed, and I worked less than two hours on several occasions, but I never took an entire day off. It wasn't something that I'd set my mind to do. There wasn't any particular reason not to work, and such days just continued for ten years; that was all.

Uncle Osu was frustrated with me for working all the time.

"Why do you live like that, when you're so young?" he said.

"I'm not so young. I'm thirty-five."

"Kid, I was thirty-five twenty years ago."

Uncle Osu and I were eating at a tripe restaurant near Hapjeong Station. He had been taking me there once every couple of months, ever since my dad died. They used to go there often, he said. He ordered three portions of tripe and two bottles of soju every time. He drank all the soju. Most of the time, it was just the two of us, but sometimes he brought someone, a theater colleague, he would say. I realized only later on that these had been blind dates of sorts. He set me up with seven guys in all. I ended up dating two of them—the ones who called me afterwards and asked me to go out with them. I dated one for half a year, and the other for a year and a half. Both times, they dumped me. One said he could never tell what I was thinking, and the other said he felt like he couldn't get close to me, no matter how much time passed. Uncle Osu clicked his tongue when I told him what they said. *Kids today are so wimpy and fickle,* he said.

We finished the tripe and ordered some stir-fried rice. In the meantime, I stepped out for a smoke.

A man was flicking off his finished cigarette with his index finger. He discarded the stub in a pot and put a new cigarette in his mouth. I took out a cigarette from my pack and went up to the pot, and our eyes met.

"Huh," I said.

"Oh," he said.

After these exclamations of neither gladness nor surprise, we couldn't say anything for a while. Jing stood looking dazed, and I must have looked the same to Jing.

"You ... haven't quit?"

That was the first thing he said to me in fifteen years—what an odd thing to say.

As I stood there blinking, Jing's eyes wavered for a moment, then regained composure. He chuckled and said, "Oh, it's just that everyone's been quitting these days."

"Oh," I said, and lit my cigarette and took a long drag.

"How have you been?" Jing asked.

Slowly exhaling the smoke, I said, "I've been well. You?"

"Same with me," he said.

We fell silent for a moment.

"When did you get back?" I asked.

The Specters of Algeria

Jing flinched.

"How did you know?"

"That you left Korea?"

"Yeah."

"Pure chance."

"Pure chance?"

"Yeah."

"What do you mean, pure chance?"

"I mean exactly what I said."

Jing looked perplexed.

"Did you see my mom?" he asked.

I didn't say anything.

"No one but my mom knows that I ever left Korea," he said.

With the cigarette still in my mouth, I inhaled and exhaled, and inhaled and exhaled again, staring at Jing. My silence, and my gaze, must have told him something, for his face stiffened. His body seemed to tense as well, then he stepped up close and said in a tight voice, "Where is she now?"

*

Uncle Osu didn't see him. Jing was standing with his back to him, and turned around once to look at Uncle Osu, but he was stirring the fried rice with a wooden spoon just then, his eyes fixed to the table.

"He's gotten old," Jing said. He was looking at me by the time Uncle Osu raised his head.

"Aren't you going to say hi to him?" I asked.

"Later," Jing said after a long pause.

When I returned to the table, Uncle Osu asked me who I'd been talking to. After some hesitation, I told him that it was just a guy I knew.

"He didn't seem like just a guy you know," he said. Grinning, he started teasing me to get me to say something more, saying, *I sensed sparks flying between you two; I thought he would throw his arms around you, the way he lunged at you; Why did you stare after him when he left?* and so on and on. Failing to get any reaction from me, he studied my face, then wiped the grin off his face and scooped up some fried rice for me.

As always, Uncle Osu walked me home. Before I went inside, I sat on the front steps for a moment. I say a moment, but when I looked at my watch, an hour had passed.

I turned the key in the lock, opened the door, and went inside; she flew at me, and I nearly fell on my back. I barely managed to pull myself together, and I asked her what was going on. She was shivering all over, frightened. I helped her to the living room sofa. After calming down a bit, she told me what had happened.

She had gone out that evening and was on her way home when she saw something cross her path all of a sudden. She stopped short instinctively, and so did the thing. She took a careful look at it, under the slanted light of the streetlamp, and saw that it was a little rat. The two of them stood there, both frozen to their spots. She felt the rat's gaze. It was a gaze full of fear toward an enormous creature much bigger than itself. Slowly, and as quietly as possible, she took a few steps back, lowering herself. In a moment, the rat scampered away.

The Specters of Algeria

She shivered again, her face pale, as if the rat were right in front of her eyes. I forced her, seemingly lost somewhere back in the past, to look at me and called out to her twice: "Aunt Soi! Aunt Soi!" The doctor had told me to do that when something like this happened. *Twice?* I'd asked. With a gentle laughter, the doctor had said, *It doesn't have to be twice exactly—a few times, several times,* then added, *till her focus returns.* I worried that several times would turn to a hundred times, but to my amazement, her gaze always returned to me after I called out to her twice. The doctor had then told me to start talking to her immediately. *What should I say?* I'd asked. Anything. *What if I can't think of anything?* The doctor had laughed again. Most of the time, I couldn't think of anything to say, but I squeezed out whatever I could, which, in the end, came out as words.

"A rat is only a rat," I said.

"*Is* a rat only a rat?" she said.

"It's nothing to be afraid of."

"It *is* something to be afraid of."

"You are *much* stronger than a rat."

"That's what I mean."

"What do you mean, that's what you mean?"

"I mean, that's what makes me afraid."

"What does?"

"That it's nothing to be afraid of."

I couldn't think of anything more to say. *How long do I need to keep talking to her?* I'd asked the doctor, and the doctor had looked at me for a while, then asked if I was afraid.

Afraid of what? I'd asked.

He'd replied, *That something might go wrong with her, because you did something wrong.*

Could that happen?

The doctor had chuckled again and said, *Just keep talking to her until your mind is at ease.*

Not until her mind is at ease?

It's the same thing.

Aunt Soi sat up and called out to Jing and Yul. Jing and Yul came and snuggled up to her. Jing was a boy, and Yul a girl. She had gone out on a walk one day and brought home the kittens that had somehow ended up in a big box that reached up to her knees, all skin and bones and barely managing to let out a meow. She gave Jing and Yul a little can of tuna each and lay down on the sofa and closed her eyes. I looked at her without saying anything, then whispered to her:

"Aunt Soi."

She pushed her eyelids open.

"Yeah?"

"I saw Jing."

"Jing?"

"Yeah, Jing."

"Jing always sees Yul. Yul always sees Jing. Because they're brother and sister. Yul and Jing love tuna."

"Not the cat. I saw the real Jing."

"What's the real Jing?"

"Jing, your son. Pak Hyeonga."

"Jing" was his birth name. My dad gave him the name "Hyeonga" later. *Hyeon* means string, as in a string instrument, and *ga* means beauty. The name "Eunjo" was something that

Jing's dad gave me. *Eun* means silver, and *jo* means bird. "Yul" was the name Jing's mom gave me, and "Jing" was the name my mom gave him. *Yul* means shiny, and *jing* means clear.

*

In Jeju, she never ended up remembering who I was. She didn't recall when she'd come to Jeju, where she'd been living, or what she'd been doing there. She didn't remember my mom and dad, not even her own name.

All she remembered was Jing. She knew two things about Jing. That he was her son, and that he wasn't in Korea. It was a good thing, she said, that he left Korea.

"How do you know my Jing?" she asked.

I said nothing in reply, then asked, "Have you eaten yet?"

"Why? Will you get me something to eat?"

We left the beach and walked to the closest restaurant. They served grilled fish. She chose mackerel, and I chose Spanish mackerel. Mackerel was her favorite fish. I had eaten about three spoonfuls of my rice when she finished hers. She gulped down a cup of water and said, "Do you really know my Jing?"

"Yes."

"How do you know him?"

"We were friends when we were young."

"I see," she said, then ordered another bowl of rice and finished it in no time.

"Where do you live?" she asked.

"In Seoul."

"Can I come over?"

"Sure."

"Let's go, then," she said, getting to her feet.

"Now?"

"Why not?"

It never crossed my mind at the moment that I would end up living with her for such a long time.

She liked the house. She even named it "Soyojae," explaining that *soyo* could either mean a stroll here and there, or a disturbance created by a crowd. She also said that saying "soyojae, soyojae," out loud sounded like a bird chirping. She used my dad's room. She said she liked it because it was as quiet as a grave. I expressed concern about the lack of light, and she tilted her head as if she didn't see what I meant.

"But there's light everywhere," she said.

I told Uncle Osu about her, and he immediately came running over. He threw his arms around her the moment he saw her and burst out sobbing. She, however, didn't recognize him.

According to Uncle Osu, he lost touch with Jing and his mom about half a year after Jing's dad died. Everyone was anxious to find out their whereabouts, but no one could to the end. I said I'd had no idea, and he nodded and said, "Your dad didn't want you to know."

"How come?"

"He probably thought it would shock you."

"Do you think it would have?"

"Are you saying that there was another reason?"

"No, what I'm saying is ... would I really have been shocked?"

Uncle Osu looked at me blankly and said, "Yes, you would."

The Specters of Algeria

"Why?"

"Because it's always shocking when someone suddenly disappears."

"Is it?"

"Yes. You never get used to it, no matter how many times it happens."

I thought every day that I should have her go back to where she had come from. But there was no way of knowing where that was, and above all, she seemed to have no intention of going anywhere. I thought and thought about what to do but couldn't come up with anything, so time passed, nothing being done.

It was two months later that she finally recognized me. I was doing the dishes when she said from behind me, "What did you say your name was?"

"Yul," I said.

"Yul?"

"Yes."

"You're really Yul?"

I stopped moving.

"When did you get so big, Yul?"

I dropped the dish in my hand and turned around. Her eyes were wide open in surprise.

The Yul she remembered was from very long ago. Me that I didn't even remember, me when nothing had yet happened to us. From her stance, *that* Yul was not a memory but someone in the present. In her mind's time, my mom and dad, and Jing and his dad, were still together. She asked where everyone was. And where *we* were.

The next day, she went back to not recognizing me. She seemed to have forgotten, too, how we had met in Jeju. She did remember the house, though. She remembered that she lived there and had named the place. But she thought that it was her house, not mine.

She kept remembering me and forgetting me at loose intervals. I kept wondering what I should do.

Just once, I abandoned her. I'd been living with her for more than a year and a half. It was August, to be exact. One evening, she remembered me again, as well as everyone else. In her mind's time, we were laughing and talking, not aware of anything that was to come. My mom sang, my dad danced, Jing's dad recited poetry, and she played the guitar. Jing hummed along with the guitar, and I was asleep, my head on my mom's knees. My dad and Jing's mom exchanged a dialogue from a play. The title of the play was *The Specters of Algeria*.

"What on earth does it mean for someone to feel something about something?" Jing's mom asked.

"Do you want to be human?" my dad asked in return.

"Tell me a secret," she said.

"A secret about what?"

"About anything."

"Find a contradiction."

"If I do, will you give me a name?"

"Why do you need a name?"

"Because I need courage."

"Then I will."

"What is my name?

"Hammonia."

The Specters of Algeria

"And who are you?"

"Who *am* I?"

"Fred."

The dialogue went on and on.

The backpack she'd been carrying in Jeju had contained simple toiletries, several bank notes, and a play. A play titled *The Specters of Algeria*. I don't know if it was a printout or a copy, but the text was less than a hundred pages, and the red cover had the title and the letters "UKKU" written on it. They were handwritten in black marker, unlike the text, which had been typed. I asked her whose handwriting it was, and she said it was hers. I asked her if she had written the play, then, and she said no; I asked her who the author was, and she said no one knew who the author was. She said that UKKU was the name of a ship, a ship that had been able to go anywhere at one time but could no longer be found anywhere.

"How come?" I asked.

"Because it left the map," she said.

I had been living with her for about half a year when I read the play. I wondered if I would be able to, but to my surprise, I was able to read it to the end without any symptoms coming on, other than a stiff neck from the fear of getting a headache. I didn't know when this change had come over me.

Four specters appeared in the play, against the backdrop of a bar called "Algeria." Two of them sat at one table and the other two at another, and the two who named each other Hammonia and Fred were the protagonists. The other two broke into the conversation now and then, and the four would talk. None of them knew how they had ended up in

Algeria, why they had to stay there, and how they could get out; they would talk about other things, often forgetting that, and then someone would recall the fact and remind the others, and they would ask and answer questions, like in a chorus that was repeated at regular intervals.

Anyway, where are we?
Yes, where are we?
Algeria.
That's right, Algeria.
How did we get here?
Yes, how did we get here?
I want to get out.
So do I.
How do we get out?
Yes, how do we get out?
Can we get out?
I think we can.
When?
Now.
When is now?

Anyway, it might have been because of the extreme humidity and temperature that midsummer day, right around midday. What she was saying wasn't all that different from what I'd heard before, but each and every word of the dialogue grated on my nerves—even the breaths between the words.

A swarm of cicadas started shrieking all at once, and I couldn't take it anymore.

"That's enough," I said, quite calmly at first.

She wouldn't stop.

The Specters of Algeria

"That's enough! Please!" I shouted.

"What's wrong, Yul?" she asked.

"It's over."

"What's over, Yul?"

"Everything. There's nothing left."

"What are you talking about, Yul?"

I walked out of the house with my hand around her wrist, and she followed, dumbfounded. I don't remember how long I walked or in what direction. I just kept going as far as I could, until I was so exhausted that I couldn't walk anymore. Then I came to a stop, left her there, and started running. I don't remember how long I ran or in what direction. I just ran as far as I could, until I was so out of breath that I couldn't run anymore.

It took me less than ten minutes to get home in a taxi. As soon as I was home, I took off my sweat-drenched clothes and stuffed them in the trash, then took a shower and passed out into a deep sleep.

When I opened my eyes, the day was breaking. The world was as hushed as if it were submerged in water. The darkness out the window soon turned bluish, and I could hear people's footsteps now and then. I had heard the same sound morning and evening, but it frightened me now. It sounded as if the footsteps would change their direction all at once and close in on me.

I looked everywhere for her. I even went to the adjacent town, and the one next to that, but she was nowhere to be found. I made calls to all the police substations in the area. A couple of hours later, one of them called back, saying someone who fit her description had been found. She didn't recognize me.

"Who are you?" she asked.

"It's me, Yul."

"Who is Yul?"

"Jing's friend."

"And who is Jing?"

It was only for a moment, but it was the first time that she didn't remember Jing. I didn't panic.

"Jing is your son, Aunt Soi."

"Who is Aunt Soi?"

I pointed at her with my finger.

"But I don't have a niece."

"I'm not really your niece."

"Then who are you?"

"I'm Jing's friend."

"But Jing is my son."

"That's right."

"What's your name again?"

"Yul."

"Yul? You're Yul?"

"Yes."

"When did you get so big, Yul?"

She didn't recognize the house. She said she'd give the house a name because she liked it. The name she came up with, after giving it much thought, was Soyojae.

The Specters of Algeria

*

My mom and Jing's mom were classmates in middle school. They were in the same class the first year and became friends when they joined the drama club. They went on to different high schools and colleges but remained best friends throughout. My mom and Jing's dad went to college together. They met in a theatrical circle. My mom was a Korean language education major, and Jing's dad, a history education major. Both were more interested in playwriting than in performing and became fast friends. They could talk about everything, but they weren't attracted to each other. My mom got Jing's parents together, and soon after, Jing's dad got my parents together. My parents went on a date because they were told to, but neither of them wanted to start a romantic relationship at the time.

My dad and Jing's dad were classmates in high school. They became friends by sharing cigarettes one day. One evening, Jing's dad had my dad come over, saying his girlfriend had broken up with him. They stayed up drinking all night, went out on my dad's motorcycle at dawn, and barely escaped death when a truck came charging straight at them and they, in a split second, instinctively sidestepped it and went flying into the air. The incident added the modifier "destined" to their friendship. The two went on to different colleges. My dad was a drama major. Recognizing before anyone else that Jing's dad had a gift for drama, he tried to persuade him to change his major, but Jing's dad could not overcome his parent's opposition.

It was half a year after they had been introduced to each other that my mom and dad fell in love. He fell in love with her first. It was the day that the play written by my mom and Jing's dad was put on stage for the first time. My dad, who had come to see the play, joined the crew for the party afterwards. He fell for her when she spat out a curse at a guy who was hitting on her. It was Jing who told me the exact words: *Fuck off.* Jing had heard it from his dad. To be precise, he said we were all together when someone brought up the story, and everyone was thinking back on the moment when someone asked, *What did she say exactly?* and Jing's dad gave the answer. I was asleep at the time, and they laughed for quite a while.

Anyway, my dad, once in love, resorted to all sorts of artifices he thought would attract girls in order to get my mom's attention: an indifferent gaze, a silent demeanor, a low voice, a faint smile, an uproarious laughter, strong and resolute statements, an unexpected sense of humor, giving his full attention with a fixed gaze when someone spoke, whistling while looking bored, etc., etc. Thanks to these tricks, all the girls around him began to fall for him, but my mom didn't bat an eye. *So typical,* she thought.

"She didn't want to admit that she was drawn to what was so typical," my dad once said.

"Yeah, right," my mom said, snorting.

"You're right. That's exactly her," Jing's mom said, siding with my dad, and my mom glared at her.

"She's right, that's part of her charm," Jing's dad agreed, chuckling.

"I don't like girls who are proud," Jing interjected, and all the grownups burst out laughing and looked at me. I flushed, feeling embarrassed. My mom slapped Jing lightly on the back.

"What, are you saying that Yul has no pride, or that you don't like her?"

She said she fell in love with my dad after seeing him walk a tightrope.

He learned how to walk a tightrope for the first time when he was twelve, from my grandmother. He just picked it up by watching her, to be exact. Once in a while, my grandmother would go out into the yard in the middle of the night, tie one end of a rope to a persimmon tree and the other to a mulberry tree, and walk on the rope. One night, he woke up and saw her walking the rope and opened his eyes wide with wonder and begged her to let him try. My grandmother came down from the rope, got a knife from the kitchen, and cut the rope. My dad began to hiccup, startled by the cold severity which he had never seen in her before. A few months later, even deeper in the night, he caught her walking the rope again. This time, he peeped through a crack in the door, not making a sound. My grandmother, walking and dancing on the rope, looked like a completely different person. No, she *was* a different person, he said.

"I mean, she didn't seem human. She seemed like some kind of a particle—an ultimate unit that can't be broken down any further," he explained.

Jing's dad used the line in his play and took him out for drinks for three days straight, in payment of "royalties."

What was seared even more deeply in my dad's memory than my grandmother walking and dancing and jumping on the rope, however, was her sitting absently on the rope with her legs crossed.

"What was it like?" Jing's dad asked.

My dad made to reply, then hesitated, and then tried again; but in the end, he could only say that there were no words to describe it. He did add, though, that when he saw her sitting there like that, he would burst into tears in spite of himself. He discovered the reason for these outbursts in a passage of the play Jing's dad had written. It was something the female protagonist said.

"It seemed to reveal everything about him. But to the end, I couldn't say what it was."

This time, my dad took Jing's dad out for drinks for three days straight.

Once, just once, my grandmother taught my dad how to walk a tightrope. He had been watching her in secret as usual. After she was finished, she came down and began to untie the rope from the tree, then turned around all of a sudden. Startled, he hastily crawled under a blanket. In a little while, she came into the room and just sat there for some time, then called to him.

"Jiseop," she called out, but he didn't answer.

"Jiseop," she called again, and he just shut his eyes tighter.

"It's just this once. You can play on the rope just this once. Never even look at a rope again after this," she said.

Slowly, he sat up.

"Why not?" he asked.

My grandmother said nothing for a while, then said, "Walking the rope brings bad luck."

The Specters of Algeria

She untied the rope, then tied it much lower than she had done for herself. My dad got on the rope, and she held his hand. Overcome with excitement, he was about to start walking at once, but she tightened her grip on his hand and pulled him back, restraining him.

"Wait," she said.

As soon as he had regained his balance, he attempted to move forward again, and she clicked her tongue.

"Wait until the rope accepts you," she said.

He hadn't realized it when she'd been holding his hand, but standing on the rope by himself was no easy feat. As soon as he let go of her hand, he fell backwards. He fell again and again, dozens of times.

That was all. He never walked her rope again, or saw her walk the rope.

My grandmother, he said, was adopted into the family of the leader of Joseon's last troupe of traveling actors. My dad heard the story from my grandfather when he was twenty, a year after my grandmother died. He didn't know why he hadn't told him before, or why he'd decided to tell him then. My dad wanted to know more about her, but my grandfather didn't say anything further, as if he had said everything there was to say. My grandmother had always been scant of words, and so had he.

My dad thirsted intensely for something, something out of his reach, whether it was something that had to do with my grandmother or the rope, or his roots. In the end, he decided to learn to walk the tightrope. He was late in starting but picked it up quickly. His teacher, the top pupil of a Living National Treasure, told him that he would have become a master of tightrope walking if he had started sooner.

Fascinated by the story, Jing's dad ransacked through all kinds of history books in search of records on Joseon's last troupe of traveling actors. Thanks to his efforts, he learned a great deal about traveling actors, but he couldn't, to the end, find any records on Joseon's last troupe. It occurred to him, too, that even if he did find something written about them, there might have been another troupe of traveling actors, about which nothing had been written, the truly last one. After that, neither records nor the last troupe seemed to matter, and the only thing that remained was a desire to walk the tightrope.

According to my mom, my dad wasn't all that great at walking the tightrope. He said he could stay on the rope for a good twenty minutes, but she said he could for less than five minutes, and take no more than five steps forward, at that. Whenever both insisted that they were right, Jing's dad intervened, saying evasively that it was about ten minutes or so, and seven or eight steps. Anyway, my mom was at once captivated by my dad. She couldn't take her eyes off him as he barely managed to take one difficult step after another, drenched in sweat and his arms flailing frantically in an effort to keep his balance. She shuddered with thrill at the sense of danger, a possibility that he could fall to the ground and never return to where he had been, the power of concentration that arose from the sense of danger when all he had to rely on was the rope, his complete absorption into which nothing in the world, it seemed, could penetrate.

The Specters of Algeria

But one day, my dad said to her, "You've never loved me, not for a moment. I know. I just know."

"Neither have you, you bastard," she said in return.

It had been raining all day. She had come home a couple of months after he burned all the paper in the house, and several months had passed since. That day, they threw dishes at each other, slapped each other in the face, and not satisfied with that, they smashed the furniture. They were quiet for a few days after that, then they began to pick on each other again, and hitting each other, and breaking and smashing things. Sometimes, they burst into tears after fighting. She would start crying first at times, and he would at others, but in the end, they both cried. The crying would start hysterically, in a high-pitched scream, then grow drier and weaker, turning into what sounded like the echo of a low-pitched wind instrument, and stop when it turned into moans that came flowing out with regular breathing. Then the two would pass out and sleep for ten hours, twenty hours.

Things kept repeating themselves.

I would stare blankly at the beige wall, which had once been the earth. When I stared and stared, the continents, islands, and borders that had disappeared beyond the wall reappeared one by one before my eyes, and lying down, I would reach out my index finger and trace their outlines in the air. I thought that maybe now, I could draw a world map as nicely as Jing.

I wanted to call Jing whenever the fights became extreme, but held back. I kept holding back, then one day, I did call him. He picked up. *Hello? Hello?* he repeated several times, then after a long pause, he said, *Yul, is that you?* I didn't answer. *Yul,* he said. I heard a crash—my dad, or mom, must have thrown something, shattering it—and I hung up with a start. About an hour later, Jing's dad came over. I was sitting huddled in a corner of the vanished earth when he opened my door and called my name.

"Yul."

I burst into tears.

Jing's dad came up to me slowly and stroked my head, then held me gently in his arms.

"It's okay, Yul. It's okay," he said, and I soon calmed down.

My mom and dad were now in hand-to-hand combat. He held her by her wrists, and she spat in his face after struggling to get free. Jing's dad jumped between the two, trying to pull them apart, but was knocked down by a blow on the chin from my dad. He shouted, "Enough, you fuckers, that's enough! Yul's watching! Yul's watching, I said!"

The two stopped for a moment. He let go of her wrist, and she sank to the floor. So did he. They sat there like that for a long time, panting. Slowly, their breathing quieted down, and I thought the fight had come to an end. But in a moment, he turned around to look at Jing's dad, then glared at my mom, saying, "You slept with him, didn't you?"

"You crazy son-of-a-bitch," my mom said.

"I know everything. I just know."

"Yeah, right. You don't know anything."

He pounced on her again. Jing's dad quietly got to his feet and closed the door to my room.

Curses and crashes continued for some time. Then everything stopped at once. I fell asleep, then jolted awake after a bit. I stared at the wall and the ceiling for a long time. I was hungry. I opened the door and didn't see anyone—not my dad, or my mom, or Jing's dad. The living room was clean, as if nothing had happened. Jing's dad must have cleaned everything up. I opened the doors to the other rooms. My dad was asleep in one, and my mom in another. I closed the doors quietly.

I went to the kitchen and opened the fridge. There was nothing but eggs to eat. I pulled out a frying pan from the cupboard, put it on the stove, and cracked a couple of eggs into it. I sprinkled salt and pepper on them. I put the two fried eggs on a white plate. I sat down at the table and ate them. They were good. After I was finished, I made a couple more, and placed them on two separate plates, then went back into my room and slept some more.

Two years later, my mom died. It was pancreatic cancer. She died six months after she was diagnosed at the hospital. Three years after that, Jing's dad died, from liver cancer. *Cancer was the trend in those days,* Uncle Osu said once, while chewing on tripe. I smiled, thinking it was a joke. Uncle Osu placed the chopsticks, which had been hovering over the grill, neatly down on the table, and said, lowering his voice, "I'm not joking. There are certain periods of time when everyone dies for the same cause."

*

When she saw Jing, Aunt Soi sank to the floor.

"Why did you come back?" she asked.

Jing took one slow step after another and came to sit down in front of her.

"I came to see you," he said.

She burst out sobbing. Jing put his arms around her shoulders. She fell asleep crying in his arms.

That was all there was to their reunion.

Jing got up quietly. I did the same and saw him off. I was going to go out just to the main street, but Jing stood still with the taxi door open, then turned around and said hesitantly, "Won't you come with me?"

My mind went blank.

"Come with me," Jing said, pulling my hand. In reflex, I stepped down hard on my soles.

"Wh-where?" I stuttered, and Jing stared blankly at me and broke into a soft laughter.

"To the airport, where do you think?" he said.

"Oh."

We passed through downtown, and I thought I saw the horizon between the land and the sky, and then I was looking at the horizon between the sea and the sky; and then when I saw a boundary line far off in the distance, I wasn't sure if it was between the sea and the sky, or the land and the sky. The sun was setting, and clouds of multifarious shapes were floating in the sky. They kind of looked like mold.

"Pretty," I said.

The Specters of Algeria

"What is?"

"The clouds."

Only then did Jing look out the window.

"They're cumulus," he said.

"Huh?"

"The clouds."

"Oh."

Looking at the cumulus clouds that resembled mold, I wondered: Why did I hesitate, when I'd go anywhere if he asked me to? Where would he have taken me, if I said I'd come with him? What kind of a place is it?

After checking in, Jing turned around and smiled. My heart shrank. Jing was startled.

"What's wrong? You look pale," he said.

"I'm cold."

"In the middle of summer?"

"Too much air conditioning."

Jing put his hand on my cheek.

"Your face is hot."

I pulled my face back, lifting his hand from it. His hand hanging in the air, he looked at me blankly, then grabbed my hand and said, "Come with me."

"Where?"

"Wherever."

"What do you mean, wherever?"

"To eat, or have coffee, whatever."

We went into the cafeteria and ordered a baked potato topped with whipped cream and an omelet. Potatoes were my favorite, and eggs were Jing's. Even after we ordered, Jing seemed to think there was something missing and asked for two beers as well. We didn't say a word as we drank. Jing ordered a couple more. Again, we didn't say a word as we drank.

Before proceeding to the immigration desk, Jing gazed at me for a while, then smiled and spread his arms open and wrapped them around me.

"It's going to be all right," he said.

"What is?

"Everything. Everyone."

I pushed hard against his chest.

"If everything is all right, why are you leaving? Leaving me, and leaving your mom behind!" I said.

Jing looked at me and smiled again, and stroked my head, saying, "Because both you and Mom will be all right."

"And what about you?"

"I'll be all right, as long as you and Mom are."

"What does that mean?"

Jing stroked my head for a long time, a smile on his face, then kissed me and said, "I'll come back."

"You mean it?"

"Yeah."

"When?"

"Soon."

I nodded.

I stood there for a long time after Jing disappeared through the departure gate.

Two months later, a letter came from Jing. He was working at a Korean restaurant in Finland, he said. The owners were two Finnish women who liked Korea even though they had never been there. That's why they had opened a Korean restaurant. Jing said he was hired immediately because he was Korean. He had planned on just passing through Finland but was now going to stay for a while because of this unanticipated job offer. He said that the two women were a couple, and adored him as if he were their son. They asked him if he had someone in his life, and he said he did; they asked him what the name was, and Jing said, *Yul.* They repeated my name again and again.

Yul.

Yul.

Yul.

They want to meet you. Come visit sometime.

Yes, I will, I answered, reading the letter.

I didn't write back. Jing would know that my answer was yes.

Part Two

CHEOLSU'S STORY

1

I woke with a start. I opened my eyes but closed them again right away. The light was fierce. The darkness created by the eyelids was frail. I shut my eyes tighter, as if to put up another barrier under the eyelids, but my effort was much too futile to defeat the light which had already seized power over the earth and the sky. The light wasn't hot, though.

My consciousness failed to connect the present to the moment before I fell asleep. My body sensed gravity but failed to figure out what the place or the hour was based only on the faintly detected temperature or smell. Recalling space and time is something the consciousness does. It's the body, however, that brings the consciousness to the present.

A rough sensation at my hands drew half my consciousness, straddling on the edge of my dreams, to my body. My consciousness answered the call of my body. It was sand. I was lying on sand.

I opened my eyes. The light wasn't as fierce as I'd thought. Perhaps the initial shock had prepared my eyes to embrace the light. Contrary to my expectations, the light was soft and languid.

The coast was empty.

I wondered if that was how it had looked before I fell asleep. I couldn't remember.

I shifted my gaze and saw someone standing there with their back exposed. Was it someone I knew, or not? Was it a man or a woman? I couldn't tell. Was it because of the distance or the sunlight? I couldn't tell. Not knowing whether it was someone I knew or not, or whether it was a man or a woman, or whether I couldn't tell because of the distance or the sunlight, I stared at the bare back for a long, long time.

Maybe it was you.

Yul.

Is that your name? Yul?

Staring at your back for a long time, I wondered if I had stared at anyone's back for so long. *Once you start staring at someone's back, you end up staring at it for a while,* I thought.

I wanted to touch it. I wanted to know what your back would feel like on my fingertip.

I lifted my hand from the sand and extended it toward the back. It met the tip of my finger. That was how it looked, at least. Eyes know nothing, as I'd always thought.

They didn't meet. If they did, my finger wouldn't have looked so big, big enough to cover your back.

My hand dropped to the sand.

I closed my eyes.

Maybe I was still dreaming. Maybe even that thought was a dream.

The Specters of Algeria

*

I had a dream. I was lying in an extra bed in a hospital room. The patient was my father. The name of the disease, aplastic anemia.

I was thirsty. I slowly got to my feet and opened the fridge. The only thing in the otherwise empty fridge was an egg, whose expiration date I couldn't recall. I went to the bathroom. I drank and drank the tap water from the sink. Once my thirst was quenched, I had to pee. Half asleep with my eyes closed, I had a good piss that smelled like last night's soju; I pushed my eyelids half open and felt a chill and shivered. Something darkish caught at the edge of my vision. I opened my eyes completely and turned quickly around, and saw a black bird, the size of a pigeon, staring at me from a corner. I froze. The bird, too, stayed fixed to its spot, then it started moving just its head, up and down, left to right, then wriggled its feet, and suddenly spread out its wings. I clenched my eyes shut, and opened them again. The bird was gone.

I opened my eyes. It had still been a dream. I was lying in an extra bed in a hospital room.

I had dreamt of a black bird before, many times. An enormous black bird would be covering up the sky; a regular-sized black bird would be sitting on a wall; or dozens of black birds would be sitting all over a zelkova tree with bare branches. They weren't nightmares, exactly, but after one of these dreams, I always felt down all day, as if the air pressure were low.

The first time I had a dream about a black bird was about

a month after my father had been hospitalized. That day, I had gone to the hospital with some cold buckwheat noodles. Cold buckwheat noodles were my father's favorite food.

"Beware of the black birds," he said out of nowhere.

"Never say anything back when a black bird talks to you," warned my father gravely, and picked up some noodles with his chopsticks and slurped them up. I stared despondently at the top of his head, which was empty save a few strands of white hair.

It wasn't the first time that he had said something that made no sense. According to his doctor, it was a sort of delusional symptom, seen in patients who had difficulty coming to terms with their disease. According to my mother, he said these non-sensical things because he was upset over the verdict drawn by the Korea Workers' Compensation and Welfare Service that despite the strong possibility of him having been exposed to a solvent that caused the disease while working at a semiconductor factory, his illness couldn't be deemed a result of industrial accident because there wasn't sufficient evidence. His doctor told me to pay close attention to him when he spoke, and my mother told me to pay no attention. At times I did as the doctor said, and at times as my mother said.

That day, I was following the doctor's advice so I ended up asking, "What happens if I say something back?"

"What do you think happens? You end up having a conversation" was my father's reply.

"Well, what happens when you have a conversation?"

"The conversation continues on and on."

"Is that all?"

The Specters of Algeria

"You say that as if it's no big deal."

"Everyone has conversations."

He stared at me with a bewildered look on his face, as if I were the one saying something absurd, and took a sip of his soup.

"So then, what kind of a conversation do you end up having?"

"About this and that. Just a random conversation."

He smacked his lips, frowning at the bitter taste, it seemed.

"And you don't like these conversations?"

"I don't."

"What don't you like about them?"

"I don't like how they go on and on."

"What's wrong with that?"

"Just think, that something goes on and on without ever coming to an end. You'll get a splitting headache."

"Then why don't you just not have these conversations?"

"It's not so easy. When someone talks to you, you end up reacting somehow, in some way—you start thinking or feeling, which makes the conversation continue. For example, say that you and I are talking like this, and this bird says something to us. You'd want the guy to stay out of it, because you don't want things to get confusing. So you tell him that it would be better if he stayed out of it, and he'd say immediately, *So, what are you talking about?* And so ..." he paused and made a sound like either a moan or a dry cough.

"So you mean ... even now?" I asked.

"That's right."

"He doesn't stop, even for a moment?"

"It's not like that. He's quiet a lot of the time. But this

wretched head, it starts thinking, *It's quiet—is it over?* And then without fail ..."

"The conversation continues."

"Yes."

"He just talks, without making an appearance?"

He looked at me, his eyes narrowed, and pointed in my direction with his chin.

"He's on the top of your head—he's been there for a while."

My father passed away within the year from a cerebral hemorrhage. If he had held out a little longer, my life might have changed its course. The prolonged hospitalization had depleted his severance pay and savings in no time, and I had decided to give up on theater and find a job. Being the only son, I couldn't go on living as I had if I were to take care of my mother who was left on her own, but things took an unexpected turn. My mother said that she would go live with my aunt, who ran a bed and breakfast in Yeosu, where she was from. My aunt was happy that my mother was coming home, as she, too, had lost her husband a few years before. I tried to keep her from going, but she insisted.

"I'm exhausted. I just want to lean on someone, even if it's just for a while."

"You can lean on me."

"What do you have for me to lean on?"

"I'm going to live differently from now on. I've already made up my mind."

"Well ... we'll talk again then."

To me it sounded like she was saying, *I don't trust you.*

2

The day I went to see Tak Osu was the forty-ninth day after my father died. It was also the day that Lee Sedol had his first match with AlphaGo. Contrary to people's faith and expectations, Lee Sedol was defeated by AlphaGo. I don't have the slightest idea what the game of go is about, and have never had an interest in it, but I was quite depressed nonetheless to hear that he had lost. Depression turned to fear as I read some Internet articles talking about what his defeat meant. I felt that I should do something, but didn't know what. Feeling anxious, I downloaded a go app on my smartphone for no good reason. I played for a while, and then quit.

A week earlier, I had called my mother on the phone to discuss the forty-ninth day memorial rite. She told me that she had converted to Christianity and said that we would not be having either a forty-ninth day memorial rite, or any memorial rite from now on, for that matter. I hadn't seen that coming.

"If you must do something, do it on your own," she said.

"But ..."

"But what?"

I felt exasperated. My mother always went straight for what she wanted once she'd made up her mind, no matter what. My father had never been able to put up with it, but it hadn't bothered me because I just thought that that was how she was; but at that moment, I couldn't understand her for the life of me. Did she really have to make such an abrupt decision? And did she have to cut me off so cold-heartedly once she'd made her decision? It wasn't as if the fate of the nation rested on it.

"I mean …"

"You mean what?"

I couldn't tell her what I was thinking. If I did, I would be reproaching her for the way she had lived her entire life; I didn't want to start a belated argument, turning my life over when I had always tolerated the way she had lived her life, especially now that my father's life had come to an end.

"Couldn't we at least hold a remembrance service?"

"You mean a memorial service."

"Well, they're …"

"They're different."

"Oh."

I was going to ask if she planned on holding a memorial service, but didn't. Whether it was remembrance or memorial, a rite or a service, what I really wanted to say was something else, so everything besides that would, in the end, mean nothing. Just as she had said, if I wanted to do something, I would just have to do it on my own.

I did nothing. I thought about going to the charnel house, but that wasn't where my father really was, and with that thought in mind, I no longer wanted to go. I spent the morning mulling, *Shouldn't I do something? But what should I do?* Then I happened upon the match between Lee Sedol and AlphaGo. I felt depressed, then afraid, and when the sun went down, I felt a pang of hunger. I had ramen and eggs at home, but I felt like a good, solid meal, so I went out.

Where I ended up going, though, was just a noodle place. I took my time studying the menu, with the names of all kinds of noodles on it, and ordered a bowl of cold buckwheat noodles.

"Do you want it to go?" the owner asked.

"Huh?"

"You usually order hot noodles when you eat here, but you always get cold buckwheat noodles to go."

"Oh, I don't like cold buckwheat noodles. They give me stomach pain."

"Huh?"

"Cold food doesn't agree with me."

"Oh. Well, then ..." the owner lady said, smiling awkwardly, and I finally saw where the conversation had gone wrong.

"Cold buckwheat noodles, please. For here."

I was about halfway through the noodles when *the woman* opened the door and entered. The dream, which I had forgotten about, came flooding over me. I wasn't sure if she was the bare-backed woman in the dream, but my face flushed, as if I had sneaked a peek at her naked body.

She sat at a table diagonally across from me and ordered cold buckwheat noodles.

"Cold buckwheat noodles are popular today," the owner said, looking over at me. The woman followed her gaze and glanced at me. I got a hard-on. What the hell was the matter with me?

Pretending that I was absorbed in eating, I finished the bowl in no time. I was wearing loose sweatpants, of all things, so I didn't dare stand up; I had no choice but to order another bowl of noodles. When the noodles were served, the woman finished eating and left. I pretended to take a few more bites, then got up and left as soon as my hard-on went limp.

I looked on my way home and saw that the lights were off in her shop. The closing hours were irregular. They probably depended on the amount of work each day.

Yul Alterations.

The sign was old, the words made up of acrylic pieces cut up using a knife and a fretsaw. I liked the words, in a font I didn't recognize. In this day and age when there's a font called "Cursive Script," and people hardly ever write something in their own handwriting unless they're doing calligraphy, the words looked like a letter, handwritten by someone just for me.

Once, I asked her what her name was, for the first and the last time. She looked at me blankly, as if she were hearing someone speak a completely foreign tongue, and lowered her head.

"Is your name Yul, by chance?" I asked.

She raised her head and looked at me with the same blank look on her face.

"Oh, it's just that the sign says 'Yul Alterations' … My name is Kim Cheolsu, by the way," I said.

She looked at me some more, then lowered her head again, and went back to the sewing machine.

Thinking back, I recalled that my face had flushed then as

well, and that I'd gotten a hard-on. Again, my face flushed and I got another hard-on. I ran home, as if to flee.

When I got home, though, I felt relieved, thinking that it was nothing to be so ashamed of, then I felt empty inside for some reason.

Picturing her, I masturbated. I felt even emptier.

I took some soju out of the fridge, poured it into a half-liter beer mug I had stolen from a bar, and sat down at my desk. I felt as if I should do something of great importance but didn't know what, so I just sat there, idly surfing the Internet and emptying the mug sip by sip.

I opened the fridge, thinking I'd have another bottle of soju, but there wasn't any left. No soju? I had run out of cigarettes, lighters, and water before, but never soju. I ransacked the cupboards, confident that there had to be a bottle somewhere. There wasn't. I fell into terrible despair, as if I had lost everything I owned, even though there were still hundreds of millions of bottles of soju in the world, and I could easily get one if I just stepped out through the front door. I knew I was being silly, but I couldn't really laugh.

I felt ashamed of myself, as if I had no right to drink any soju that existed in the world ever again. And then I felt ashamed of everything about myself. I felt ashamed before my father, ashamed before my mother, ashamed before the woman, and ashamed before the world. Soon, I might feel ashamed before a machine.

Feeling ashamed, I sat back down at my desk. I surfed the Internet out of habit, then clicked off the page with a start. I had no time for this. I really had to do something. But what?

Anything.

I decided not to do anything until I thought of something.

One hour passed, perhaps two, or maybe even three, which would surprise me. Then the name flashed through my mind.

Tak Osu.

Mirae, an older girl who used to be in the same theater company with me, had mentioned him once. That was the first time I heard the name. It was the day that the director— the head of the company—had announced that we would disband, giving in to financial pressure. We sat drinking all night, pledging that we'd drink for three days straight, drink to our death, but as the sun came up people started leaving one by one, until only Mirae and I were left. Her tongue was twisted, and my ears deafened. We sat there griping about the traitors who had broken their vows, then we both had a vomiting fit and sat there in silence afterwards, depressed.

I asked her what she was going to do from now on, and she said she had no choice but to go on doing what she'd been doing.

"What are *you* going to do?" she asked.

I had nothing to say in reply.

"Quit the theater, if you can," she said.

"Why should I?"

"Don't you know why?"

"How come you're not quitting, then?"

"My life is as good as over, but you're still young."

She finished her cup, and I finished mine after her.

"Quit ... and go where?"

"Why are you asking me?"

The Specters of Algeria

"Who else can I ask?"

She stared at me for a while, then finished her glass again.

"Tak Osu."

"Huh?"

"Ask Tak Osu."

"Who's that?"

"You don't know Tak Osu?"

"Should I?"

She shook her head, as if to say I was hopeless.

"Your dream is to direct, and you don't even ... I knew you were ignorant, but where is the limit of your ignorance?"

"Oh, come on, just tell me who it is."

"Tak Osu, I said."

"So who is this Tak Osu?"

"A genius."

A chuckle escaped me.

"What, you're one of those genius worshipers? You?"

This time, she chuckled.

"I thought you were just young, but you're a baby."

"Oh, please. I'm only six years younger than you."

We went on with this silly argument over age, then began to find fault with each other's gender, then jumped from one topic to another, raising our voices, laughing, clapping our hands together, getting snippy, one crying, the other laughing, then both singing together. The soju kept pouring endlessly.

When I came to myself, we were in a motel room. We were lying side by side, buck naked. I turned my head only slightly, but she sensed the movement and slowly opened her eyes.

I didn't know what to say.

"Do you even remember what happened?"

I didn't.

She wrapped herself in a blanket and sat up. I quickly got her a bottle of water from the fridge. Chuckling, she took the water, drank it, and put a cigarette in her mouth.

"I remember it all," she said.

"Huh?"

She chuckled again.

"I'm saying, you didn't abduct a passed-out girl and then rape her."

"Oh …"

What a relief.

"I'm sorry," I said nevertheless.

"For what?"

"For not remembering."

We left the motel and went to have some soup for our hangover. I had beansprout and rice soup, and she had ox blood soup, with a bottle of soju as well, after which we went our separate ways. I came home and slept for fifteen hours straight. I might have slept some more if my mother hadn't woken me up to eat.

It was about half a year later that I came across the name again. I had been hired as a contract worker in the planning department of a theater run by a community cooperative. While helping a theater company put on a show, I ran into Yunho, a guy I had worked with in the directing team of another theater company. Yunho, a production assistant at the time, was now a director, and even appeared on stage at times as an actor. His role was to run in the background in slow motion from one end of the stage to the other, for the forty-some minutes the play was performed. He didn't have any lines, but he was applauded as much as the lead actor after the performance. The key, he said, was to divide up the distance, which would take about ten steps to cover walking with shoulder-width strides, by forty and then move forward, maintaining the average speed as precisely as possible. He said he practiced over a thousand times to get used to the pace. I nodded, saying, "I can see why. Really, that character was a stroke of genius."

His eyes crinkled in a mysterious smile as he asked, "In what way?"

"I'm not sure if I should put it this way … but if not for that character, the whole play would've been too ordinary," I said.

He let out a long whistle.

"Pretty impressive, kid, that you caught that," he said.

"No, you're the one who's incredible. That character was your idea, wasn't it?"

That's when the name popped out of his mouth. Tak Osu.

It turned out that Yunho was friends with Tak Osu's nephew. So they all ended up having a few drinks together. After he finished writing the script for the play, he sent it to Tak Osu and asked for his feedback. It was the first script he had ever written, and he was going to decide whether or not to put it on stage depending on what he said. Tak sent a reply, with the brief comment, "A little too straightforward," along with the advice, "But since you've finished writing it, find a way to put it on stage. It would be better if you added a character who has nothing to do with the plot. A guy who just runs quietly on the stage all through the play, for instance."

At first, I didn't remember the name. I just kept thinking that it sounded familiar somehow, and when Yunho started talking about something else, I forgot about it. Then as we were talking about people we knew and what they were up to, Mirae's name came up, and it finally hit me.

"Is this person a genius?" I asked immediately.

"Who? Mirae?"

"Tak Osu."

He was raising his cup of soju, but stopped for a moment, then took a drink.

"Is that what Mirae said?" he asked.

I didn't answer him.

"She's the only one who would say something like that," he said.

"So he's not a genius?"

"Why are you asking me? Decide for yourself."

I told him I didn't know him.

"Your dream is to direct, and you don't know Tak Osu?"

Again, I drank until dawn and slept for fifteen hours, and forgot about the name.

Tak Osu.

I put his name in a search engine and pressed enter.

He was a director and playwright. He had directed twenty-five plays, for sixteen of which he had written the script himself, and had scripted fifteen other plays. There weren't that many articles on him. Most of the articles that did exist just provided information about the performances; he had never done an exclusive interview, and nothing had ever been written about his personal life. I felt relieved, thinking that he wasn't *so* famous that everyone should know him. I learned through someone's blog that he had retired from the theater world after putting his last work on stage nine years before and gone to Jeju soon after to open a bar. It said on someone else's blog that the name of the bar was "Algeria," and that the title of the last play he had put on stage was *The Specters of Algeria*. The play, it seemed, was his most famous work, both for the directing and the script. He staged it a hundred times over a period of twenty-some years and quit the theater completely after the last performance. I wanted to read the script but couldn't find it on the Internet.

I called Yunho. It had been a year since that day I ran into him. He didn't pick up.

I called Mirae. No answer there, either.

I left them both the same message, asking how they were and if they had access to the script of *The Specters of Algeria*.

About an hour later, Mirae texted back.

I'm not sure. Anyway, it's good to hear from you.

I was about to text back *Thanks anyway*, when she texted again.

Yunho says he's not sure, either.

So they were together. I wondered why they hadn't picked up the phone, and why she had texted back for him, then grew annoyed and closed the screen. She texted again. She was drinking with a bunch of people, including Yunho, and said I should come join them if I wasn't doing anything. They all wanted to see me, she said. I felt better, and felt for a moment like going, but declined in the end. I didn't want to see her again in this slapdash manner.

It didn't take long for me to find everything written on Tak Osu and read it all. The last thing I read was a bachelor's thesis titled "A Study on the Theater of the Absurd in South Korea—with a Focus on *A Conversation Between Two Long-necked Men* by Pak Joyeol and *The Specters of Algeria* by Tak Osu." Considering that the analysis on Pak Joyeol was very general and skimpy, the review on *The Specters of Algeria*, full of nothing but praise, probably wasn't that credible, either.

Not wanting to break the flow of concentration, I pulled out two collections of plays written by Pak Joyeol, which I had bought several years before in a secondhand bookshop, and read them from cover to cover. Some passages I even recited out loud.

And then—there was nothing more to do.

I felt even more despondent and restless than before.

Should I go join them for a drink? I wondered.

I went out thinking that I would, but I let three or four taxis pass by and went to a convenience store and returned home with two bottles of soju instead.

I went on an Internet music site on my smartphone and put "Introitus" from Mozart's Requiem on endless repeat, and began to drink. "Introitus" was the title of the first short story I wrote, when I was twenty years old. A panel, consisting of students in the creative writing department, evaluated the story and said that it was more like a play than a novel; I wrote more than twenty short stories after that, but they all received similar feedback. Over the course of several years, I submitted twelve short stories in all for the annual spring literary contest, but none of them made it through even the preliminary round. At the advice of an upperclassman in the department, I turned one of them into a play and submitted it, and this time, it won. I got excited. It felt as if the entire universe had turned into a finger, and was pointing at me, saying, *You're the one!* After military service I joined the drama club at school and began to work toward my dream, learning about the theater one thing at a time. Experiencing the powerful sense of reality that arose from the sharp conflict between, and the exquisite fusion of, artificial virtuality and primitive realism, I became more and more enamored with the theater. Writing plays alone wasn't enough; I wanted to be in charge of all the precarious but perfect moments created by the stage as a whole. That's why I came to dream of being a director.

Achieving the dream wouldn't be easy. Even the prospect of becoming a playwright was remote, let alone a director. Even if one of my plays were put on stage, or I made my debut as a director, my circumstances wouldn't improve all that much. The glory days of drama were long past, with no chance of revival. The era does not look back on things whose time is up. It's always a few individuals who make the effort to retrace them so that they're not forgotten, but in the end, even they grow exhausted. It isn't just in the theatrical world that great achievements are gradually consigned to oblivion. That was simply reality, as I was learning from reality. It could well be a miracle that any achievement is able to live on at all. But it's always a *person* that creates a miracle, and that's why I was confused, unable to decide whether or not to quit the theater.

The finger of the universe was still pointing at me, though.

The reason why you haven't achieved your dream lies in you. It's because you didn't make an effort, because you're not a genius, because you're unlucky, the universe was saying.

So I shouldn't blame my circumstances. Yes, that, too, must be my reality.

From my smartphone continued a song sung for the dead by believers of God:

May they have eternal rest. May they have endless light.

I finished both bottles of soju and listened some more to "Introitus."

Why don't they ever sing for the living? I wondered for the first time.

The answer came quickly: *Because it's a requiem.*

But the one for whom the song was intended could not hear it. Those who did hear the song were not the one for whom it was intended. Who was the song really for?

Would I be the one for whom the song was intended, or would I be the one to hear the song? If I wanted to be neither, who should I be? Or, who was I?

Ask Tak Osu, Mirae had said.

He's a genius.

I turned off the music and booked a flight to Jeju. I planned to meet Tak Osu and ask him: What does it mean to be alive?

What must you do if you're alive? Besides dying?

3

It was a little past two in the afternoon when I arrived at Algeria. There was a small sign on the closed door that said: Open at five p.m.

I booked a room at a bed and breakfast nearby and headed to the beach. It was almost deserted, maybe because there was no sand, or because it was off season. I walked for about an hour and saw only three people pass by, with long intervals in between. They looked like tourists, from what they were wearing.

Hungry and tired, I went into the first café I saw. I ordered an Americano and waffle set and ate it while watching the sea stretched out before me. I asked for another round after a while. I was told that there were free refills on the Americano, so I just ordered two waffles instead. After I finished I still had some time, so I went out for another walk. I didn't run into anyone this time.

Algeria opened at five forty-five. I was sitting on the patio chair by the door when a woman who looked to be in her forties approached and glanced at me, then opened the door with a key. She went inside, leaving the door open, and I went in after her. She turned around, and I hesitated. She smiled.

"Sit wherever you want. The menus are on the tables," she said.

The space was rectangular, almost square in shape, about twenty pyeong. There were six tables in all. Across from the entrance was a counter and a bar, and behind the bar was a shelf full of records. To the right was the kitchen, with a sink, a little cooking table, and a fridge, and to the left were two large windows. I sat at the table by one of the windows.

As the woman had said, there was a menu on the table with the names of thirty or so items, most of them liquor, written in black marker. The last line read, "Side dishes vary depending on the ingredients of the day."

The woman was doing the dishes in the kitchen, with her back to me. It seemed it would take some time for her to finish, as there were piles of dishes in the sink and on the counter. As I sat waiting for her to finish, she turned around and asked, "Would you like something to drink first, or to eat?"

"Oh, please, take your time," I said.

"Thank you," she said in a pleasant voice tinged with a smile.

Looking out the window, I watched the sun go down. The sun set completely while I was lost in thought for a moment. In the meantime, the woman had griddled a kimchi pancake and put it on the table.

"It's on the house. You can take your time with your order," she said.

"Thank you. I'd like a beer, please."

For three hours, I sat there drinking three bottles of beer and a bottle and a half of soju, as well as eating steamed clams and boiled pork slices. The pork was on the house, too. She couldn't take money for it because she had prepared it the day before, she said. There were seven slices in all, but they were thick slices and looked close to half a pound. Feeling full, I left three slices uneaten. While I sat there eating and drinking, four groups of people came and went. The last group, consisting of two women in their thirties or forties and three men, seemed to be good friends with the woman. From what they were saying it sounded like they, and the woman, and Tak Osu had had a party there the night before, one that had lasted until early in the morning. Tak Osu, it seemed, couldn't come out to the bar that day because of a hangover. They called him Mr. Tak.

*

What does it mean to be alive?

A line from *The Specters of Algeria*.

It means that you're not dead.

The author of the thesis wrote that those lines were at the core of the main theme of the work and symbolized hope. According to the quoted passage, the subsequent dialogue went as follows.

That's something even I could say.

Then do it.

Do what?

Say what you said that even you could say.

But it's not mine.

Then don't.

Why shouldn't I?

Why shouldn't you what?
Do what you told me not to do.
Do it, then.
Do what?
Anything.
I'll draw some water.
Yes, go on and do it.

The one who replies is A, and the one who asks, B. A is an old man who is writing something titled *The Specters of Algeria*, and B is a young man who keeps drawing water out of one well and filling another with the water, and when that well is full, draws water from it and fills the first well with it.

There are two other characters: C and D. They keep watch on A and B. C and D talk mostly about what A is going to finish writing. They say that A's work would provoke B, and B would stop drawing water in the end. They guarantee that this is a very dangerous thing, but don't know why it's dangerous. A forgets what he is writing from time to time, as if he has dementia. About halfway through the play, A runs into the watchers, and the watchers tell him what he has forgotten. As they talk to A, they even tell him what he will be writing in the future, and A writes down what they tell him. Eventually, A finishes what he's working on, but the watchers steal the work and burn it to keep B from reading it, and A forgets that he has finished what he's been working on. As the four continue to do what they've been doing, the play comes to an end. The author of the thesis writes that although nothing happens in the end, the fact that A and B continue to do what they've been doing means that they will not disappear,

The Specters of Algeria

and the fact that they exist, in itself, is a form of resistance, as well as a source of terror. That's why those two sentences symbolize hope, according to him. I thought that either the author didn't understand the Theater of the Absurd, or that *The Specters of Algeria* wasn't an absurdist play.

*

I woke up to the sound of my cell phone ringing. It was my mother. She said she was at my place in Seoul. I told her I was in Jeju, and she screamed, "What on earth are you doing there? You left this place looking like a pigsty!"

She was sobbing. Quietly, I listened to her cry. She calmed down before long. She said she'd put some food in the fridge and told me not to skip meals, and hung up without waiting for my reply. I looked at the clock, which said 10:37 a.m. I stayed in bed a little longer, then washed up and went out and had breakfast at a restaurant nearby.

It was a little past two in the afternoon when Mirae called. I was walking on the beach. She asked me where I was and I said Jeju; after a pause she asked, "You didn't go to Algeria, did you?"

Her voice had dropped all of a sudden.

When I told her I did, she screamed, "Why would you go there!"

I was stunned at first, and then a mixture of feelings swept over me. *What is wrong with everyone?* I thought.

"What's it to you ..." I said, trembling all over.

Then raising my voice, I spat out, "... whether I came here or not!"

"Well, you ... better not say anything to him about me," she said, relenting a little.

"What would I say about you?"

"You wouldn't have gone there just to read *The Specters of Algeria* ... Well, anyway, don't even tell him that you know me."

Vague assumptions flashed through my mind.

"Why aren't you answering me?" she said, raising her voice again.

"What do you think I'm here for, then?"

"That's what I'm asking! What are you doing there?"

She sounded anxious. I, however, grew calmer.

"I only learned just now, from you, that you know him personally," I said.

"Just now? For real?"

I couldn't tell whether the problem was that I hadn't realized something had happened between the two of them, or that on some level I had.

I didn't say anything, and neither did she. That was the end of the conversation.

*

"My name is Kim Cheolsu. I was in the same theater company with Jeong Yunho," I said, introducing myself to Tak Osu.

"Jeong Yunho? Jeong Yunho ... I don't recall," he said.

"He directed *A Hundred Years Ago Today*," I said.

The Specters of Algeria

"A Hundred Years Ago Today …"

"I heard that you took a look at the script for him. You commented that the work was too straightforward … and that's why you advised him to add a guy who ran …"

"Oh! Yes, I remember. A friend of my niece's."

"Yes, that's right."

"So you were in the same theater company as him, huh?"

"Yes."

"Are you an actor?"

"No, I was in the directing team."

"Who was the director?"

"Kang Teukchul."

"Kang Teukchul? Kang Teukchul … Oh, Kang Teukchul! Isn't his real name Sky, or Mountain, or something?"

"It's Sea."

"Yes, Sea. Kang Sea. The little kid has become a director, huh?"

"Yes."

He laughed, clapping his hands, and drank some soju. I filled his cup again, and we toasted and drank together.

He filled my cup, asking, "So, what brings you here?"

"Well, I … came because of *The Specters of Algeria* …" I said.

"What about it?"

"I want to read it."

He finished another cup in silence.

"You mean the script?" he asked.

"Yes."

"I don't have it."

"Oh, then if you could tell me who does …"

"Why do you want to read it?"

"Well … I …"

I couldn't tell him that the desire had come over me out of nowhere. It had in fact come over me out of nowhere, but nothing ever really happens without context. There was the forty-ninth day memorial rite, for instance, and AlphaGo, and buckwheat noodles, and the girl at the alteration shop, and the finger of the universe, and Mirae. Wait, not Mirae. Anyway.

"It's a long story …" I said.

"A story can only be so long. It couldn't be as long as life," he said.

It *could* be as long as life, actually. If I started arguing over the context, everything would turn into cause and effect, and if I started tracing cause and effect, my own birth would be the first of all the causes. Wait, no, it wasn't as if I fell out of the sky one day …

"You're thinking too much. Just spit it out, anything. Once you do, it'll all come together," he said.

"Well, the thing is …"

"Oh, come on. Start by telling me what you did before you came here."

"Here?"

"Here, Algeria."

"Oh. I took a walk on the beach."

"And before that?"

"I had something to eat."

"What did you have?"

The Specters of Algeria

"Beansprout and rice soup."

"Was it good?"

"It wasn't bad."

"And before that?"

"I talked to my mother on the phone."

"What did you talk about?"

"Nothing much."

"You must have talked about *something.*"

So the conversation continued, and I ended up saying more than I'd expected. The words branched out, at first in chronological order, then according to topics. I didn't go all the way back to the moment of my birth, but I had never said so many things out loud about my past before.

The last thing I talked about was the first story I ever wrote. He asked me why the title of the story was "Introitus." I told him that I couldn't come up with a good title even after finishing the story, no matter how I tried, so I downloaded several movies at random to divert myself; the background music in one of the movies kept going around in my head, so I looked it up and learned that it was Mozart's Requiem, and when I downloaded the album on the Internet and did a further search, I learned that the title of the first section, "Introitus," meant a short prayer sung before Mass and used that as the title of my story. And I liked the sound of it, too.

"Tell me how the story goes," he said.

The story was about something that believes itself to be an earthbound spirit in an old shopping district building, which is about to be demolished, tracing the tenants of the building one by one, certain that he was murdered by someone even though he doesn't remember it, to find out why he'd been killed and who he'd been before he died.

"That doesn't sound bad. Why did your friends say that it was like a play?" he asked.

"Because there wasn't much of a description or narration," I said.

"So that's what kids who write novels think of plays."

In trying to make an excuse for them, I said, "They also said that the dialogue had a dramatic rhythm." Realizing that I had just praised myself, I flushed red.

"Dramatic rhythm? What's that?" he asked.

I shouldn't have said anything, I thought.

"I shouldn't have asked. Never mind," he said, and raised his cup in a toast.

"To the pain you took to come this far," he said.

I clinked my cup with his and gulped down the drink. Putting the empty cup down, I felt something cave in, and my eyes grew hot in spite of myself.

*

I woke up to the sound of my cell phone ringing. It was Mirae. She asked me right off if I was still in Jeju. I said I was, and she asked after a pause:

"Did you see the woman?"

"What woman?"

"The one who lives with him!"

"Oh … she lives with him?"

"So you *did* see her."

The Specters of Algeria

"Are they married?"

"I don't know."

"You don't?"

"No, I don't."

It all clicked together now; everything she'd said about him, and the way she'd behaved, made perfect sense.

I sat up slowly. The clock read nine fifteen; it was morning.

"Mirae," I said.

"What?"

"Do you love him?"

Once out, the words sounded like a cliché. I should have asked casually, *Do you want me to see if they are?* She would've laughed at me, for sure. But still.

"It's all in the past," she said.

I was surprised at the seriousness of her tone. It wasn't like her.

"Yeah?"

"Yeah."

I thought about asking her why she cared, then, but didn't. It was pointless to nitpick on words when it was plain to see how someone felt.

"Mirae," I said again.

"What?"

"Why don't you come for a visit?"

"What for?"

"Just come. This is my first time in Jeju, and it's great."

"That's all right. I gotta go."

I took out a bottle of water from the fridge and drank it at once. Then I opened the window and put a cigarette in my mouth. *Why do people let themselves fall in love? I wondered. When they don't even know what love is.*

Again, the thoughts sounded like a cliché. But.

I meant them.

I couldn't remember how I'd returned to the bed and breakfast, or how late I'd stayed out drinking with Tak Osu. I remembered that we'd gotten down to talking about *The Specters of Algeria,* but I was plastered by then so I couldn't recall specifically what we'd said. I think I talked about the plays I'd had a part in and the scripts I'd written until I blacked out, and he talked at length about Dolsoe. Dolsoe was the name of his dog—a white puppy born to the mongrel next door. He shared story after story about his dog and moved on to another subject only after the woman tried repeatedly to get him to stop.

I remembered now. The woman had called him Uncle Osu. Her name was Han Eunjo. I thought about texting Mirae and telling her that they weren't married, at least, but didn't. There's no law against calling your husband Uncle. And even if they weren't married, I didn't think knowing that would make Mirae feel any better.

A text arrived from an unknown number.

Let me know when you're awake.

Another text arrived soon after.

It's me, the owner of Algeria.

I called her; she was startled.

"You're up already?" she asked.

"Uh, sure," I said.

"You seem full of energy," she said, and told me to come over and have something to eat to ease the hangover.

The Specters of Algeria

I declined once out of politeness, then accepted when she asked again. She gave me directions based on where I was, so the two of them must have brought me to the bed and breakfast last night. Only then did I remember that she hadn't had a single drop of liquor. The last customer left around the time Tak Osu and I had drunk about five or six bottles of soju, and she joined us after she had cleaned up the place; I offered to pour her a glass, but she said she didn't drink.

They lived about ten minutes' walk away. A shabby one-story house of about twenty-five pyeong stood on a lot of about fifty. A basalt rock wall, the kind I'd seen only in pictures, surrounded the house. I pushed open the blue gate, stepped inside, and saw a small vegetable patch in the yard. A white dog came out of nowhere and blocked my path, jumping around all over the place. It was Dolsoe. When Han Eunjo came out, the little dog clung to her. In the meantime, I made a run for the house.

He was sleeping in a room.

There was a small, round portable dining table laden with bowls of rice with beans, bowls of beansprout and dried pollack soup, and plates of summer radish kimchi, seasoned bean sprouts, stir-fried potatoes, and rolled omelet. I wolfed down my rice before she had finished even half of hers. She offered me another bowl, which, too, I finished.

"I'm sorry to be such a nuisance ..." I said.

"Not at all. We were brought together for a reason, weren't we?" she said.

I was a bit thrown off by the unexpected warmth.

"Thanks to you, I've learned a lot more about the girl. Thank you," she added.

The girl. I had no idea who she was referring to. Just how wasted did I get last night?

Hesitantly, I admitted that I didn't remember much, and she gave a small laugh and said, "That's okay. Uncle Osu's the same way. I was talking about Yul Alterations."

"Huh?" I said, completely at a loss.

"We had a good laugh over Cheolsu and Yeonghee, the quintessential storybook names, remember?"

I felt even more lost.

"You said that you wanted to know the name of the girl at Yul Alterations."

I did. I'd told the girl that my name was Kim Cheolsu, and asked her what her name was.

"It's Yeonghee. Jin Yeonghee," Han Eunjo said.

"So that's ... um ... uh ..."

"Yul is *my* name. I owned the shop. I left it to Yeonghee five years ago and came to live here."

"But you said your name was ..."

"Yul is my childhood name. Last night, or this morning, I should say, Uncle Osu called me Yul all of a sudden; that was why you brought up Yul Alterations. I don't really like that name, though. Uncle Osu usually calls me Eunjo, but he starts calling me Yul whenever he gets drunk ..."

*

Yeonghee's father had been Tak Osu's classmate in middle school. Tak Osu was coming out of the theater after the ninety-eighth performance of *The Specters of Algeria* when a man

The Specters of Algeria

approached him, greeting him with the words, "Hey, Osu!"

People he didn't really know often said hello to him, so he was just going to give a slight bow and pass by, but he stopped dead because he hadn't been called in such a way in a long time.

The man's name was Jin Jeongsu. He claimed that they had been in the same classes during their first and second years in middle school. Tak Osu didn't remember.

Jin Jeongsu had happened to see a theatrical poster on the wall while walking down the street one day. The title of the play was *The Specters of Algeria*. Written in red letters on a pitch black background, without images of any kind, was the copy, "Specters Do Not Die." The title was in yellow. What caught his eye more than anything else was the name of the director. It was a name he had long forgotten.

In his first year of middle school, Jin Jeongsu had been planning to kill himself. He hadn't actually intended on dying. He had been trying to come up with something that he could choose purely through his own will; a cut-off place which would be beyond anyone else's reach. Death only came to his mind as a result. He felt that if he had a haven of his own, right in front of his eyes within reach wherever he was or whoever he was with, he would be fine no matter what happened. He began to read books at random so that he could round up as many examples of death as possible. He even looked up dissertations at the national library. The words didn't all make sense, but the act of reading itself had become a way of his life by then, and he couldn't stop.

What had first compelled him to do this was his older

brother. His older brother was always angry. He was only twenty-one but had long believed himself to be a failure. A failure at what, exactly, was a mystery. It seemed that perhaps he himself didn't know, which angered him even more. His days consisted of beating someone up or getting beaten, or breaking something. At times he regretted his misdeeds and resolved to start a new life, but it was all in vain. Jin Jeongsu couldn't tell whether he lived like that because he was used to being a failure, or because his way of life was the only thing that let him forget that he was a failure. On days when he came home without venting all his anger, he kicked the dog; when the dog died, he began to beat his own brother.

Their father, who was a background actor, was often absent from the home for days, and their mother practically lived at a certain church whose backyard was supposed to be home to a source of life-giving water, so there was no one to stop his brother from doing what he did. Jin Jeongsu tried talking to his parents, and spent as much time outside as he could, but his brother grew all the more vicious. He said that he hated the weakness displayed by his younger brother who dared not face him head on and defy him. Then he began to claim that it was their father who had made him that way. Their father, a helpless alcoholic who spent his life longing for the time when he had been a child actor in the limelight, had passed his blood on to them; because of that filthy blood, they had been destined to live on the fringes of society ever since they were born, never taken any notice of. In the end, Jin Jeongsu's brother left home to change his destiny after slashing himself all over with a razor blade, never to return.

The Specters of Algeria

Jin Jeongsu wondered: What, then, was the first thing that had caused his father to live the kind of life he lived? And what had given rise to that first thing? In this way, Jin Jeongsu searched one by one for the things that had led to the current consequences. There was an endless number of factors connecting one cause to another. In the end, he realized that no one was at the root of the causes, and as a result he was able to keep himself from hating anyone. But by that time, his life had become an atrocity about which nothing could be done. To free himself from who he had become, he would have to rewrite the history of all mankind. He felt as if he were about to be crushed by the load of the countless causes and consequences, with his hands and feet tied. So he began to ponder a choice that would involve only his own will from beginning to end; and he concluded that it was death.

The discovery thrilled him. He couldn't believe that the way to free himself from all those overlapping factors that had their derivation in one another had been so close within reach. He wanted to revel in the experience more fully before carrying out his decision. In fact, he could accept all the causes and consequences if he were accompanied by death, he thought.

It was as this new world of his was unfolding in its fullness that Tak Osu came onto the scene. A few months had passed since the beginning of the second semester. The two had never spoken a word to each other till then. That day, Jin Jeongsu had been sitting on a bench under the wisteria reading a book titled *Real Stories from the Emergency Room*. It was lunch hour. He always bought a cup noodle or a roll from the cafeteria because he never brought lunch to school, but that day, he had neither money nor an appetite. He didn't recall how Tak Osu had ended up sitting on the bench next to his, and what he'd said to start the conversation. Actually, it wasn't even a conversation at first. Tak Osu said things to him now and then, and Jin Jeongsu remained silent, just nodding a few times. Then Tak Osu showed interest in the book he was reading.

"I've read that too. The subtitle is 'The Crossing Point of Life and Death,' I think," he said.

Jin Jeongsu was a bit rattled. He wasn't sure if it was fear he felt, or excitement. Perhaps it was both. Tak Osu came and sat down next to him.

"To be honest, I've been reading all the books you've checked out from the library. I didn't mean to at first. I saw your name on the card in a book I happened to check out, and after that happened three times, it triggered my curiosity. Two of the book cards only had your name on them. So I decided to play a game—a game of guessing which book you would read next."

To figure out what kind of books Jin Jeongsu liked, he had to find out which books he had read until then. First he tried to find the common link among the books in which he had found his name: *The Tale of a Game of Dice at Manboksa Temple*, *The Feast of the Psychopaths*, and *My Struggle*. They weren't enough to reveal Jin Jeongsu's taste in books; the only common thread Tak Osu could see in them was that they were written by male authors, and other such trivial facts. So next he tried to take a look at the books that were connected in some way to each of the three books. *The Tale of a Game of Dice at Manboksa Temple* was a book about a scholar in the early Joseon era, but he categorized it as a classic Korean novel; *The Feast of the Psychopaths* was a book on psychology, but he put it down as a book about geniuses, and so on. It wasn't an easy task, but at least it gave him some ideas of how to proceed. However, when he had found eighteen books as a result, he took a look at the list of titles; he had failed to find an overarching link. He decided not to resort to tricks anymore. He would look through all the books in the library. This time, he would check the dates the books had been loaned as well. Thus, he found a total of one hundred and twenty-seven book cards with Jin Jeongsu's name on them. Among the books were ones that had been loaned after the game had started. In any case, he rearranged the list according to a chronological order, and consequently was able to find a certain pattern.

First, he learned that there was a keyword, "death," since Jin Jeongsu had read books with the word in the title, in alphabetical order. Then Jin Jeongsu had gone on to read books in whose table of contents, preface, author's note, and commentary, death appeared as the main theme, also in alphabetical order.

Having explained thus far, Tak Osu heaved a sigh and said:

"It got really complicated after that. The rest of the books weren't in alphabetical order, and they didn't seem to have any sort of keywords, either. So I went back to the first method. From there I learned that they were related to the ones you'd read up to that point: books written by the same authors, or books used as references by them, or ones that had been mentioned in the books. And that more recently, you've been rereading the books you read in the past. Finally, I was able to guess correctly that next you were going to read *Real Stories from the Emergency Room: The Crossing Point of Life and Death*."

He seemed genuinely happy. He even punched Jin Jeongsu playfully on the shoulder. To which he reacted by asking him if he didn't have anything better to do and jumping to his feet. To be honest, Jin Jeongsu was completely stupefied. He had never had anyone take such wholehearted interest in him. Tak Osu apologized, his face serious. He said that he had simply wanted to tell him how happy he was to have cleared a difficult game; he hadn't at all taken his act of reading lightly. Without saying anything in reply, Jin Jeongsu headed toward the classrooms in a flurry. Tak Osu quickly caught up with him and began to talk about the sixty-seventh novel Jin Jeongsu had read, saying that he had been quite impressed by the female character, "X." X was someone who suffered from unilateral spatial neglect, a neurological disorder that disabled her from perceiving the space to her right. For her, the space to the right didn't exist, even though she hadn't lost her sight.

"You know, if I came down with the syndrome, and found that out through someone, how would I prove to myself that the space exists? Or, if all of us came down with the syndrome, how would we know that half of the world existed beyond our awareness?"

How immature, Jin Jeongsu thought. The question had to do with nothing more than curiosity that could be played around with in the realm of imagination, and Jin Jeongsu, faced with a life-or-death crisis, could not afford to take part in such games. Apart from that, though, he had to admit that he began to think more and more about Tak Osu from then on. He kept noticing him, like a scratch on a pair of glasses. If the scratch bothered him, all he had to do was take the glasses off, but by then, the fact that something bothered him was grating on his nerves. It meant that the point of the matter was not the realization that he had experienced a rupture— subtle as it was—due to the intrusion by Tak Osu but the awareness that his world may not be as impenetrable as he had believed. In other words, whether or not he was ignoring Tak Osu was no longer the point. If only for the future, he had to face and deal with this first rupture head on.

Tak Osu was someone whose presence was so powerful that Jin Jeongsu couldn't help wondering how on earth he had never noticed him before. He wasn't that big of a guy, but he was taller than most kids their age, and his booming voice and knack for setting the tone of a gathering were more than enough to draw eyes to him. And above all, Pak, an upperclassman dubbed "the legendary fist," was always mellow for some reason when he was around him, so everyone in the school knew who he was. Jin Jeongsu, too, had caught a word or two about some guy, but realized only now that Tak Osu was the guy that they'd been talking about. There were other reasons, too, of course, that people flocked to him. His affability when talking to someone, and his ability to focus on what the other person was saying, were sure to touch anyone's heart.

But even after he had finished observing him, Jin Jeongsu

felt that he was too immature. He seemed kind of silly—a popular guy who constantly demanded other people's attention; Jin Jeongsu concluded that the game that had so captivated him was just another attempt to draw attention to himself. It was only later that he realized that he'd already had that conclusion in mind from the beginning, but in any case, he came to believe that Tak Osu's intrusion wasn't that fatal to the relationship between death and himself.

Even after that, Tak Osu asked him from time to time what book he was reading; but as Jin Jeongsu remained silent, he gradually stopped talking to him. Then one day, Jin Jeongsu began to reread the book Tak Osu had mentioned to him that day they first spoke. He slowed down when he came to the part about X. *What if you were me?* X seemed to be asking. The question stayed in his mind until after he had turned the last page. Jin Jeongsu, who had devoured texts that had been born out of death, as if to replenish himself with nutrients, failed to absorb the next book.

After the final exam of the second semester, Jin Jeongsu called out to Tak Osu as they were leaving school and told him out of nowhere that he had thought over the question. Tak Osu caught on right away, saying that he, too, had been thinking about it, and asked him if he had come up with an answer. After some hesitation, Jin Jeongsu replied that he hadn't been able to.

"I tried to imagine but couldn't get any further. There was nothing I could do but negate the question, telling myself that it didn't make any sense. It annoyed me in a way, but then I ... felt a bit scared."

The Specters of Algeria

Tak Osu clapped his hands, just once. Jin Jeongsu felt nervous, not sure what it meant. He had, it seemed, unconsciously hoped that Tak Osu would agree with him. The two walked on in silence. Then Tak Osu stopped cold and said, as if mumbling to himself, "Yeah, that's it—I was scared."

"Why does it scare us?" Jin Jeongsu asked, and Tak Osu clapped once again, and burst into laughter.

"That's what I was about to ask," he said.

His laughter continued on, and a thin smile slowly spread across Jin Jeongsu's lips. He realized in that moment that he, too, had a friend now.

Tak Osu remembered him at last. He couldn't believe that he had ever forgotten that name. Just as he had been Jin Jeongsu's first friend, Jin Jeongsu had been his first true friend.

But it *had* been more than forty years, after all. There must be other things that he had forgotten completely, without even being aware that he had, as though they had never existed in the first place. Time flies, but life is surprisingly long.

Jin Jeongsu disappeared a few days before their last winter break in middle school. No one in his class knew what was going on with him. To them, his sudden disappearance didn't seem a big deal. Tak Osu went to see Jin Jeongsu's homeroom teacher but was told nothing. "You're friends with him?" The teacher asked, three times. Tak Osu asked for an address and a phone number, but the teacher just stared at him for a moment, then said, "You can't be friends with him."

"What?" Tak Osu asked.

"You two are on different paths to begin with."

He persisted regardless, but the teacher was adamant, saying, "You say you're his friend, but you don't even have his address or phone number?"

One night, he sneaked into the teachers' room and looked up his friend's address and phone number on the school register. He checked them only to find that they were both incorrect. The phone number didn't exist, and living in the house were people who hadn't even heard the name "Jin Jeongsu."

"What happened with you back then?" Tak Osu asked.

Jin Jeongsu emptied his cup in silence, with an odd smile on his face.

"My brother died. Or to be precise, I killed him," he said.

Jin Jeongsu had gotten into a physical fight with his brother, who had returned home one day out of the blue. His brother instantly knocked and pinned him down, strangling him. He struggled desperately to get the hands off his neck but wasn't strong enough. He grabbed whatever his hand first came to and swung it in the air; then in a moment the clutch loosened, and his brother fell backwards. Jin Jeongsu passed out. He learned later during an investigation that he had thrust a pencil into the pressure point in his brother's neck. It was ruled that his actions had been in self-defense, so he wasn't sentenced to prison.

Why didn't you come to me? Tak Osu was about to ask, but stopped himself.

"How have you been?" Jin Jeongsu asked.

"What do you think?"

Jin Jeongsu gave a chuckle.

"I'd never have guessed that you were in the theater business."

The Specters of Algeria

Tak Osu chuckled along and asked, "You don't think it's for me?"

"I don't know, but …"

"But what?"

"I did think that you'd make a good writer."

"You're the one who said you were going to write."

"I did?"

"Yeah."

Jin Jeongsu had three straight shots of liquor and chuckled again.

"So that's why she's making all that fuss about being a writer," he said.

"She?"

"I have a daughter. Her name is Yeonghee. Same as her mother who died as soon as she had the girl. She died giving birth to her. The woman loved me a lot; the first who ever loved me like that, but she died. So I named the girl Yeonghee. Whenever I called out the name—*Yeonghee, Yeonghee!*—I felt like I could stop myself from wanting to kill the girl, since I couldn't kill Yeonghee. So I call out her name dozens of times a day, even now. Every day. *Yeonghee, Yeonghee!* Even if she's not there in front of me, I call out the name— *Yeonghee, Yeonghee!* But even so …"

Jin Jeongsu had another three shots and let out a quiet laugh.

"Listen, friend. Do you know how easy it is to kill a man?" he said and went on laughing softly.

"What's really difficult is dying. I thought that would be the easiest, but as it turned out, it wasn't," he said, then stayed silent for a long time.

The cups emptied more and more quickly.

"She's a quiet girl. She isn't interested in studying, doesn't have any friends, stays cooped up in her room doing who knows what. Then one day, she said she was going to be a writer. *A writer in this family?* I thought, but I guess it didn't just come out of nowhere," he said.

Tak Osu couldn't drink very much, which was unusual. His friend drank seven bottles of soju in just two hours. The snacks were nearly untouched.

Before they parted, Jin Jeongsu threw his arms around him.

"You're still my friend, right?" he asked.

"Of course I am," Tak Osu replied.

After getting into the taxi, Jin Jeongsu rolled down the window and said, "You know, the play, *The Specters of Algeria*. It was my tenth time seeing it today, actually, but I couldn't really see what it was getting at. Is it saying that life has meaning, or not? And what's it saying that we should do? But I guess that's because I'm so ignorant."

And that was the last of it. Contrary to his promise that he would come see the play again, he never showed up at the theater after that, and they lost touch.

It was in Tak Osu's fourth year living in Jeju that a letter came from Jin Jeongsu. He had sent the letter to the theater where *The Specters of Algeria* had been staged, and after going from one person to another, the letter finally reached Tak Osu. The letter was very brief.

Please take care of Yeonghee for me, it read.

He had sent the letter two months before. Tak Osu went to the return address on the envelope. His friend had long died;

Yeonghee greeted him. Tak Osu asked the cause of his death and she replied, "Is there a reason for someone dying?"

He handed her the letter and she took a long look at it, as though reading something very lengthy, then folded it, put it in the envelope, and handed it back to him. He told her she could keep it if she wanted, but she shook her head and said, "He didn't send it to me."

At a loss for words, he just sat there. Yeonghee sat quietly as well; then she brought him a cup of coffee.

"Thank you for coming. But I'm an adult, and don't need anyone's help. Besides, I don't even know who you are," she said.

Tak Osu slowly finished his coffee, then got to his feet. Before leaving the house, he asked Yeonghee for her cell phone number, but she refused to give it to him.

"It's not you I'm worried about; it's me," he said.

Yeonghee stared at him, her face devoid of expression.

"You don't know how hard it is to live with a heart full of regrets."

Yeonghee's face remained expressionless.

"When you don't know what someone's talking about, just do as the older person says. Didn't your father teach you things like that?" he said and handed her his cell phone.

After a moment's hesitation, she pressed her number. He hit the call button and checked to make sure that her phone rang. Then he said, "My name is Tak Osu. Text me once a week. If you don't know what to say, just write 'Hi, I'm doing fine.'"

Yeonghee didn't say anything; he barked, "Understand?"

After a moment of reluctance she said, "Yeah."

*

"And? What happened to her after that?" I asked.

The door flew open and Tak Osu came out of the room. He looked blankly down at me with his eyes half closed, then burst out laughing.

"You're still talking about that?" he said.

Han Eunjo laughed along.

"You asked that already, earlier this morning," she said.

Darn it.

She set the table a second time. Meanwhile, he took a shower and fed Dolsoe, the dog. My gaze drifted from one thing to another as I waited for the interrupted story to resume. He sat down to the table, asking, "Are you dying to hear what happened to her?"

"Uh, well …" I faltered.

"I don't know, either, other than that she's doing fine."

"Is she really?"

"I haven't heard anything besides."

"Oh."

"If you're so curious, why don't you go ask her yourself? was the last thing I said to you."

I felt myself go limp.

"What kind of a man are you, always so quick to lose heart?" he said.

Having washed all the dishes from the previous round, Han Eunjo came to sit with us, saying, "He said you can drop his name if you feel awkward just going and talking to her."

"Oh, no, it's all right," I said.

The Specters of Algeria

"Why don't you get some sun first? Nothing will get you back on your feet like the sun. It's very nice out today," Tak Osu said.

So I stepped out into the yard. And of course, Dolsoe lunged at me. As I bumbled around, not knowing what to do, he shouted from the other side of the window, "Open the gate for him if he's too much to handle!"

Before the gate was even completely open, Dolsoe made his way out through the crack and disappeared out of sight.

As I'd been told, it was very nice out, though I felt more sluggish than ever, not energized at all.

I put a cigarette in my mouth and lit it, and sat on a wooden chair, a one-seater, in a corner of the vegetable patch. The chair's center of gravity kept moving from left to right, either because the legs were all different lengths or because the ground wasn't very even. Abandoning myself to the subtle rocking of the chair, I lazily watched the curious curves created by the cigarette smoke, instantly appearing and disappearing. All around me it was hushed, as if I were underwater.

I felt as though I could stay and live in Jeju forever. With everyone—those I have lost, those I haven't yet lost but will eventually lose.

Part Three

OSU'S STORY

1

Karl Marx, the German philosopher, left France in February of 1882 to go to Algeria. He was sixty-three at the time. Since the passing of his wife Jenny two months earlier, his health took a rapid turn for the worse; it got so bad that he began to vomit blood, and his friend Engels suggested that he go to Algeria to recuperate, thinking that the mild Mediterranean climate would help alleviate the symptoms. The doctor who had been treating Marx for the pleurisy and bronchitis from which he had long suffered—as well as the insomnia that resulted thereby—was of the same opinion. Algeria was renowned in France and England among holidaymakers at the time.

Marx stayed at the Hotel Victoria in Algiers, the capital of Algeria. The hotel was located on a steep cliff, so it wasn't very expensive. On top of that, the air was clean and the view quite beautiful, which drew in recovering patients who stayed for long stretches of time. Marx stayed for three months.

Marx spent most of his time in his room or taking walks. When he was in his room looking out at the Port of Algiers, surrounded by the Mediterranean Sea, and the summit of the snow-capped mountains of Djurdjura in Kabylia, he could forget for a moment that he was a patient. In such moments he felt that he might be able to work on the second and third volumes of *Capital,* as well as the revised edition of the first volume, but in reality, he hadn't recovered at all. His respiratory condition was deteriorating from the weather in Algiers, which had never been so bad, and from the extreme temperature range. The doctor who had been called in from town advised him to refrain from extended hours of reading and writing, and to stop taking long walks. He also advised him to avoid chatting with people as much as possible; that wasn't too difficult, as most of the people staying at the hotel were arrogant and pretentious British scholars and aristocrats. It was quite an ordeal, though, to hold himself back from reading. He would have rather died than fritter away time, wasting money without doing any work. To fight the sense of shame, he tried to muster up some willpower, but his coughing fits would leave him delirious. He recalled the last words his wife had spoken before she died: *Karl, I feel so weak.*

Reading the paper and writing letters were all he could do. He usually wrote a letter every three or four days. Most of the letters were for Engels, but he also wrote his daughters Jenny and Laura now and then. When his condition became so bad that he couldn't read the paper or write letters, he contented himself by reading their letters.

April came around, and his health improved somewhat. The weather was still fickle, changing several times a day, but there were more clear days now and the temperature was generally higher. Most importantly, his fatigue from the thirty or so hours of journey across the ocean had eased at last. All it meant, though, was that he could take slightly longer walks now; his condition hadn't improved visibly. He was fed up with the unstable Algerian weather and wanted to go someplace else, but he didn't dare make another rough journey.

Taking the light rail, he would go into town now and then, paying a visit to the botanical garden or a rural village nearby. He began to write letters more often and fall asleep at night.

It was in mid-April when he began to write plays. He hadn't written one in a long time. In his youth he had written myriads of them. He had written poems and novels as well; mostly poems when he was courting Jenny, his wife. All the poems he wrote became letters for her. During their courtship they had recited the plays of Sophocles or Goethe to each other. Jenny loved Shakespeare and wrote critiques on plays after marrying Marx. Her pieces were published at times in the Frankfurt papers. Marx loved her exquisite use of sophisticated metaphors, bold yet artless.

He hadn't intended on writing drama again. Around that time, he had quoted a famous Arabian fable in a letter to Laura, his second daughter. It was a conversation between a boatman and a philosopher who had gotten on a boat to cross the river.

PHILOSOPHER.   Boatman, do you have a knowledge of history?
BOATMAN.   No, sir, I don't.
PHILOSOPHER.   You have wasted half of your life, then. Have you studied mathematics?
BOATMAN.   No, sir.

PHILOSOPHER. You have wasted more than half of your life, then.

At that moment, a strong gust of wind capsized the boat, and the two fell into the water. The boatman shouted out.

BOATMAN.   Do you know how to swim, sir?
PHILOSOPHER.   No!
BOATMAN.   Then you have wasted your entire life!

Marx had quoted an existing story, but after it was written down, something prodded him to go on writing. He wanted to expand on the conversation or write another conversation between the same characters.

So Marx picked up the pen again. Once he did, an urge to write something new came over him. His intention at first was to write something the length of a fable, but after five days of writing came the realization that he had written enough for a thin volume. He had generated a tremendous amount of output, considering the rate at which he had worked in the past, but it didn't really harm his health in any way because he hadn't written with publication in mind and hadn't required extensive concentration.

His wife Jenny would have been happy to see him writing something new, though she might have criticized him sharply, saying something along the lines of, *Karl, I don't think you'll make any money writing plays, so why don't you just concentrate on writing* Capital?

But you loved my plays, he would have countered.

That's right. And I always will. But the readers aren't me.

The Specters of Algeria

She would have looked serious and sounded firm. But she would have been delighted to see another play he had written.

He missed her.

Marx decided to send it to his daughter Jenny. Jenny loved whatever it was he wrote, never criticizing it in any way. In that respect she was both like and unlike her mother.

My dear Jenny, he began, and felt glad that he had named her after his wife.

He wrote about the weather, his health, and other aspects of his life in Algiers, then as he was about to start telling her about his play, he realized that he hadn't given it a title yet. There had been times when he made changes to titles afterwards, but he had never finished writing something without coming up with one. On top of that, he had completely forgotten that he hadn't thought of a title. He must be experiencing cognitive decline. He felt ashamed and distressed.

He had great difficulty coming up with a title for the play. He read it again three times, from the beginning to the end. He was able to correct some errors, polish his writing, and add some footnotes in the process, and the manuscript became a little longer as a result. He couldn't let his daughter see all the traces of the revision, no matter how much she loved everything about him, so he copied down the entire play on new sheets of paper. Even after all that work, though, he couldn't think of a good title for the play.

He decided to go for a walk. He walked for what seemed like an endless time, then it occurred to him that he should go back to basics. To the first sentence, for instance. He had penned it without much thought, but since the play had its beginning in the sentence, he felt that the answer lay therein. The first sentence of a work—whether the author is aware or not—is bound to determine the essence of the entire work, and at the same time reveal the initial motive for writing it. So the first sentence would give him an idea of a title.

The first sentence read as follows.

In Algeria live four specters.

A title materialized immediately.

The Specters of Algeria.

Marx ran straight back to his hotel room and wrote the title at the top of the first page of the play and put the manuscript in an envelope along with the letter he had written Jenny.

He summoned Lily. Lily was the niece of Madame Rosalie, the owner of the Hotel Victoria, and cleaned the rooms as well as ran errands for guests.

The sun was setting by then, and it was too late to go into town where the post office was, so Lily decided to send the letter the next day. Such things happened often, and no one ever complained about a letter being delayed a day. Lily put the envelope in the front pocket of her skirt and finished her evening tasks.

After returning to her room, Lily took Marx's letter out of her pocket; then she realized that the envelope wasn't sealed as usual. Lily had wondered from time to time what the guests at the hotel wrote in their letters, but having been taught that reading other people's letters without permission was an despicable thing to do, she resisted pulling out the letter and reading it, even though the deed would leave no trace, and lay down to sleep.

She had trouble falling asleep. It wasn't because she particularly wanted to read the letter. She often had sleepless nights. She usually managed to fall asleep before dawn, but that night, she remained wide awake until the day broke. Getting up from the bed, she sat down at the desk. The desk faced the window. Chin in hands, she watched the sun rise. As it happened, the sky was exceptionally clear that morning. Lily's eyes grew wider and wider. Never before had she witnessed the sun spreading its wondrous light and dispelling the darkness. She felt as if she could hear the sound of angels singing, praising the glory of God, ringing through the air.

Oh! she exclaimed, and her right hand dropped to the desk. Her fingertips touched something, its texture different from that of the desk. She fingered it without realizing, then looked down at it after the gray of the daybreak lifted completely. It was Marx's letter. Seized by a sense of wonder and feeling that she was in a pivotal moment, Lily took everything that came to her in that moment to be fate. She could have been deluded. But she thought that even a delusion, in that moment, would be fate. Without hesitation, she opened the envelope.

She discovered that Jenny Longuet, often the recipient of Marx's letters, was the name of his daughter. From the different last name, Lily had surmised that the woman, certainly not his wife, might be his lover. She had suspected an affair. He must have fled here, she'd thought, because he was caught by her husband. Or perhaps the woman wasn't of age yet, and he had left home because her parents had demanded hush money from him, using his social position as their leverage. Or maybe he had run because the girl—married or too young, or even if she was a perfectly respectable girl—became pregnant and he was afraid. All the scholars who stayed at the Hotel Victoria were neurotics, all cowardly somehow without exception, and lewd and twisted as could be, even though they were quite famous—supposedly—in Europe. The lot of them acted high and mighty, as though they could swallow Lily whole, despite the fact that they lacked the physical strength to even seduce her. They tried to lord it over her by using sophisticated vocabulary she couldn't make head or tail of, then turned purple with rage when they saw that she was thoroughly unimpressed; then they called in her aunt, Madame Rosalie, and roared that she was an impudent girl and had to be disciplined. But they probably masturbated at night picturing her naked body.

Lily *had* noticed that Marx was a bit different. He never called for her unless he had a letter to send, and when they ran into each other he simply said hello and didn't look her up and down with insinuating eyes or try to patronize her using philosophy and poetry. Just once, he had stopped her and asked how old she was.

"Fifteen," she had replied.

"Very good," he had said.

That was all. He had nodded slowly, then passed by her and walked out of the hotel. She had turned around and looked at him for a moment. She was about to tell him to take an umbrella with him because it looked like rain, but didn't.

The letter itself was only two pages long. On the next page began the play he had talked about in the letter. Lily wasn't very familiar with the German language yet, so she couldn't understand half the letter. She had taken up studying German a year before. Although she knew French and English and didn't have a problem talking to guests, a German scholar in his fifties who had stayed at the hotel once scolded her for not understanding German and advised her aunt to teach her properly. That was after he had asked Lily for a massage, handing her some money, and she had refused, saying that she didn't know how to give a massage. He had once asked her at what age Algerian women began to menstruate. *Until what age are Germen men curious about such things?* She'd retorted, and he had burst out laughing, his face flushing red. Lily was fully aware of his eyes stealing a glance at her calves under her skirt in that moment.

Madame Rosalie, unaware of what had taken place, told Lily that the scholar had decided to give her free German lessons and that it was a great opportunity. Lily flatly refused, saying, "I have no interest in learning German."

She had lied. She *did* want to learn German. She knew that his offer was only a pretext for achieving his end; but it hurt her pride. She didn't want to be insulted in such a way. It was much more awful than being disgraced for not being good at her job or for being lazy or ill-mannered; and if she couldn't come right out and say that, she didn't want to let it go on and be an excuse for insulting her.

A few days later, Lily had gone into town on a mail errand, then stopped by at the bookshop and bought a book: *Germany. A Winter's Tale* by Heinrich Heine. The owner of the shop, at Lily's request, translated and read out all the titles of the German books on the shelf, and she had liked that one the most. It sounded like the title of an exquisitely beautiful story. The owner seemed quite amazed that such a young girl was looking for a book written in German. The way she said, "I'll take that one," her eyes sparkling, was lovely as could be. Wrapping up the book, he asked her what it was for. She told him that she wanted to learn German, and he gave a quiet laugh, fell into thought for a moment, then asked:

"Do you speak French?"

"Yes."

"Can you read it as well?"

"Yes."

He pulled out a book from the shelf and handed it to her. It was a book written in French. Lily saw that the title was *Germany. A Winter's Tale.* She shook her head.

"I don't have the money," she said.

"You don't need to pay," the owner said in reply.

"Excuse me?"

"It's for you."

"But why?"

"Because you're pretty."

She was tempted for a moment to hear that it was for free, but she didn't like how he'd said that he was giving it to her because she was pretty. She shook her head again.

"It's all right," she said.

"But you said you wanted to learn German."

"So?"

"So how are you going to learn it?"

"What do you mean?"

The Specters of Algeria

Again, the owner of the shop laughed quietly.

"You did well to choose a book of poetry," he said.

Only then did she realize that it was a book of poetry.

"They'll be easier to compare."

"Compare?"

"Put the two books side by side and read them together. So that you can see what the words mean."

"Oh."

Hesitantly, she had reached out a hand to accept the book, then raised her head and looked him in the eye. She wasn't sure if she could really trust him.

"You don't have to take it if you don't need it," he said, and was about to withdraw his hand; she quickly snatched the book from him.

"Thank you," she said.

He laughed again.

First, she read the book in French. Although she was able to read the words, it wasn't easy to understand them all. There were a lot of words she had never seen before. After some time, she dropped by at the bookshop again and asked if there was the same book in English. The owner said that there wasn't and asked her why she needed it. Lily explained her predicament, and he told her to bring the French edition next time. A few days later, he wrote down in the French edition the Algerian counterparts of the words she didn't know. In just three months, Lily memorized both the French and German editions. In the same way, she read three more books in German. She couldn't have conversations in German because she hadn't learned how to pronounce the words, but she felt that she had taken proper revenge on the German scholar somehow.

As she read *The Specters of Algeria*, Lily realized that she couldn't really say that she knew German just because she had memorized four books in the language. Besides, none of the books had been a play. She had *seen* a play, just once. It was called *Antigone*. Although nobody knew this, Lily dreamed of becoming a stage actor. A French woman named Alice had once stayed at the hotel; she was a stage actor. She was quite affectionate toward Lily. Lily's strong spirit and sharp wit, as well as her eyes that were always full of hostility, reminded her of herself when she was young, she said. Alice was the one who had taught Lily French. *Antigone* was the first play in which she'd played the lead role after becoming an actor, she said. About half a year after she returned to France, she sent Lily a letter saying that she was once again to play the leading role in *Antigone*, and that the play would be held in Algiers in about a month. She also said that they would let Lily in for free if she gave them the name "Alice" at the ticket office. So Lily got to see the play, but she wasn't able to see Alice on stage. One of the theater staff told her that she passed away fifteen days before they came to Algiers; and that she had told them to give Lily the best seat in the theater. Lily didn't cry.

It was when Antigone uttered the following words that she burst into tears.

What law of the gods have I transgressed? Why should I look to the gods anymore? What ally should I call out to, when by my reverence I have earned a name for irreverence? Well, then, if these events please the gods, once I have suffered my doom I will come to know my guilt. But if the guilt lies with my judges, I could wish for them no greater evils than they inflict unjustly on me.

These were the lines that Alice had said she loved the most. Alice had written down the lines in French on a piece of paper and given it to Lily as a gift before leaving the hotel.

Although Lily couldn't understand all of *The Specters of Algeria*, she was able to understand that it was set against the backdrop of a bar called "Algeria," and that there were four characters in the play altogether. They didn't seem to remember how they had ended up in Algeria. And a certain dialogue repeated itself, like the chorus of a song. Because there were no difficult words in the dialogue, Lily could understand that part perfectly.

Anyway, where are we?
Yes, where are we?
Algeria.
That's right, Algeria.
How did we get here?
Yes, how did we get here?
I want to get out.
So do I.

Whenever she came across the dialogue, she read the words out loud. She couldn't tell if she was pronouncing them correctly. As she read, she thought to herself: *Yes, this is Algeria.* Out of all the parts that she had no difficulty understanding, she liked the following conversation the most.

Tell me a secret.
A secret about what?
About anything.

Find a contradiction.
If I do, will you give me a name?
Why do you need a name?
Because I need courage.
Then I will.
What is my name?
Hammonia.
And who are you?
Who am I?
Fred.

She couldn't understand exactly what it meant, but it seemed like such a wonderful thing for two people to give each other a name. Above all, she liked the part that said that a name is required to have courage. She felt touched somehow to think that her own name hadn't just come to her by chance.

She wanted to read the play through from the beginning. But she had to send it to France in a few hours. Lily decided to copy it down. It took her longer than she expected, and in the end, she decided to keep the letter for just two more days. No one would know, as long as she didn't tell anyone.

Just as she thought, nothing happened. As usual, Madame Rosalie and Marx didn't bother to ask if she had sent the letter, and after two days' delay, the letter was safely received by the post office and dispatched to France.

2

It was in 1983 that Pak Seonwu discovered *The Specters of Alegria*. He came upon it by chance at a secondhand bookstore in Paris, near Sorbonne University. A high school French teacher, he was traveling in France during a vacation. That was when he learned that Marx had penned a play as well as other works. The play took up half the book, and the other half was filled with commentary. He finished the book on the spot.

The first sentence reminded him of the beginning of *The Communist Manifesto*: "A specter is haunting Europe." He remembered the sentence, having seen it quoted in an editorial, but hadn't yet read the manifesto in its entirety. The book wasn't easy to find in South Korea because it was banned there. He had bought a copy just the day before, at another bookshop. Afraid that it would be detected upon his entry into Korea, he was planning on transcribing the book during his remaining stay in France and taking the copy with him. If asked, he would tell them that he was a teacher, and that he had scribbled it out of boredom on the long flight. He thought about buying *Capital* as well, while he was at it. He had obtained a pirated copy of the Korean translation the previous year through an acquaintance of an acquaintance, but he had spotted bizarre sentences everywhere, probably mistranslations. He wanted to compare the text with the original, but transcribing the entire book seemed much too difficult, so he decided against it.

The Specters of Algeria ended with the dialogue that had repeated itself throughout the play. *Anyway, where are we? Yes, where are we? Algeria. That's right, Algeria.*

The four had failed to get out of Algeria. They never found out why they had been locked up, or what they were doing there. It was a dismal ending. It wasn't like Marx, Pak Seonwu thought. But Marx, too, must have felt somewhere along in his life that everything would come to an end as it was, nothing having changed. Questions and answers keep repeating themselves, and the heart roams aimlessly. It was a quite universal trap, one into which anyone could fall. Or was it fate? A natural destiny that no one, in the end, could avoid. Perhaps such were the things that Marx had wanted to talk about.

But a fate in which changes were impossible? Really, that wasn't like Marx at all.

The person who had written the commentary—a German author born in Algeria named Lily Müller—had a completely different take. According to her, Algeria was a refuge of sorts for the four characters in the play. Her reason for concluding thus was that none of them remembered the past; for complete rest is impossible when one still remembers the times through which one has passed. It is memory that enables people to see themselves as consistent beings, even if everything about them has changed; consequently, the greatest sense of human fatigue comes from the fact that there is no possible way of freeing oneself from that sense of self. So the four weren't trapped in Algeria; they had freed themselves from the closed-off time that was themselves. That, however, did not mean freedom. Paradoxically, freedom was something that could be attained only by re-entering that time. Only when a self—in possession of a memory of having existed as a self that had nothing to do with its former self—joined that former self could it, and the self that had been trapped in a non-self, become a self that is both itself and not itself; freedom was something that could be experienced in that process. The process could repeat itself endlessly. The more it repeated itself, the further it would push back the boundary placed on the self, and freedom, too, would increase as much; for freedom is not a finalized concept. If it were, that would mean closure, which would allow for no freedom.

The commentary was more difficult to understand than the script itself. In a way it sounded like a play on words. But it didn't seem like a complete joke, either.

It went on talking about time. To sum it up, it said: the four are specters because they have no past, which means that they have come out of finite time and become infinite beings. Their bodies feel no pain, and they would never die. In most of the scenes in the play, they laugh as they exchange what sounds like jokes to pass time, with sweet liquor and a variety of food to keep them company—as if nothing has happened. Then they realize that there are things that they don't know. They ask where they are, how they had come to be there, and give one another names. They try to put an end to their infinite rest by defining things and making an attempt to be defined, to find themselves. Because that is possible only in time, in other words, only through history. That was the way Marx loved people, the author was saying. And that it was a choice—to define and to be defined—that only those who have loved could make.

The commentary went on to discuss the circumstances in which Marx had written the play in Algeria. It was a year before he died. Marx, as seen by the fifteen-year-old Lily Müller, though reticent and quite melancholy, was always courteous and kind. It was only when she had become an adult that she learned what a great scholar he was, much more so than she had presumed. It was even later that she learned what kind of life he had lived.

Marx was always haunted by expulsion, death, and poverty. He was expelled from Germany, his own country, as well as from France and Belgium. He had seven children, four of whom he lost to death. When his third daughter, Francisca, died only a year after she was born, he didn't have the money to buy a coffin and managed to have a funeral for her only by borrowing two pounds from a neighbor. He had written a number of books and become quite renowned by his thirties in Germany, France, and Britain, but his books didn't sell well, and fame brought him no money. He frequented pawn shops to feed his family, and even worked as a European correspondent for an American newspaper at one time. Thanks to the help of his wealthy friend Engels, though, he was able to weather financial crises whenever he hit rock bottom. Crucially for Marx, he had his wife Jenny who stayed by his side through those menacing times, frightening in more ways than one. Jenny, the daughter of an aristocrat, had been brought up in an affluent home. Even as she languished in poverty, which she would have never experienced had she not met him, she never resented Marx. She always loved and respected him. He may not have been able to endure those times without her love.

He wrote the play *The Specters of Algeria* in the year following her death. The letter that Lily Müller had peeked at talked about what her death meant to him. Much time had passed since and she couldn't recall the specific words, but she vividly remembered how he had referred to himself as a "specter" in his writing. She couldn't remember, she admitted, whether Marx himself had stated that his own body was as good as gone since Jenny, who had been one with him, was gone, which meant that he was essentially dead already, or if the thought had come to her as she read his letter.

I can fill a thousand books with words; but I will fill them with only the name, "Jenny," Marx in his twenties had written to his beloved.

I close my eyes and picture your happily smiling eyes. And I'm happy that I mean everything to you, and nothing to everyone else, Jenny in her twenties had written to Marx.

The two courted each other for seven years. Even after they got married, they always wrote each other whenever they were apart.

I love you. I long for you.

Lily Müller wasn't of the opinion that they loved each other in an especially remarkable way, nowhere else to be found. And she believed that the object of one's love didn't always have to be a lover or a spouse. It could be a friend, a teacher, a brother or sister or children, or just about anyone else. What mattered was the experience of love itself. Although the symptoms of love showed up in the form of identifying oneself as the object of one's love, being one with another person was impossible in reality; so those who were in love were bound to undergo moments of severe self-dissociation, endlessly going from a sense of absolute connection to one of absolute disconnection. Embracing all those moments as something that belongs to oneself, and once again building relationships with all that doesn't belong to oneself—that was the essence of love, Lily Müller was saying. The experience of love had been stamped in Marx's body, mind, and heart through Jenny; if not for those moments of love, Marx may have lived an entirely different life, she contended. So the initial motive for all the works Marx had written for the world to read was love, and anyone who had been in love would be able to detect this love in his works.

The Specters of Algeria was published for the first time in Germany in 1923. It was Lily Müller who provided the manuscript. She had been living in Germany for almost thirty years after accompanying her husband Maximillian Müller there and was suffering from heart disease at the time; being aware that she wouldn't be able to live much longer, she resolved to put Marx's play into publication before she died. At her husband's advice, she took the manuscript to Verlag von Otto Meissner, the company that published volume one of *Capital*.

The Specters of Algeria

The head of the company was suspicious since she wasn't related to Marx in any way and had brought the manuscript no less than forty years after his death. Lily told him her story. He took quite an interest but regretted that there was no one to corroborate Lily's account; saying that he would take a look at the manuscript at any rate, he sent her home. But he didn't give her an answer even after some time had passed, so she took the manuscript to another publisher. The head of this other company happened to be an acquaintance of Charles Longuet, Marx's son-in-law, and he showed Longuet the manuscript. Longuet remembered that a letter his wife had received long ago from her father had contained a play by the same title. The letter was long lost by then, but he hadn't forgotten that it was about four specters who lived in Algeria. The head of the publisher, learning later on that Lily was an author who had already published two books of poetry and one full-length novel, put her essays together into a book along with Marx's *The Specters of Algeria*. The book became a topic of conversation for some time after some coverage in a newspaper article, but it sold less than a thousand copies. It soon faded from people's minds.

The copy that Pak Seonwu had obtained was the French edition published in 1965. He transcribed it along with *The Communist Manifesto* and brought the texts with him to Korea. Then he typed out *The Specters of Algeria* on a typewriter, made several copies, and bound them. He meant to give them out as souvenirs to his friends in Chilhyeonhoe.

3

"I never imagined that *The Specters of Algeria* was a work by Marx," Kim Cheolsu said.

My throat was dry, so I gulped down a cup of water. Yul brought me a cup of hot honey water.

"None of us did," I said.

"But ..."

"But what?"

"I read something a bit different on the Internet."

He said he'd read a thesis comparing Pak Joyeol and me. It didn't pique my interest because there had been others who had talked about the two of us under the key phrase "Theater of the Absurd," though not in a thesis.

A journalist once wrote in an article long ago that my play was from the Theater of the Absurd movement. My friends and I talked about it over a drink, making fun of the author for wanting to sound smart; but more and more people began to say the same thing, and before I knew it, everyone was saying it. The Theater of the Absurd was all the rage back then. The fad passed, and when *The Specters of Algeria* was put on stage again after an interval, the label was no longer in force.

A snort escaped me as I sat listening to what the thesis said. I'd guessed from the beginning when I heard the title, but it seemed that the guy who wrote it was even lazier than I'd thought.

"Maybe I'm wrong since I haven't read it myself, but … I think this guy has some studying to do," I said.

"About the Theater of the Absurd?" Kim Cheolsu asked.

"No, about the theater in general. And about resistance and fear. About desperation, above all. He needs to think about what it is he's most desperate for, to be exact. Studying, of course, doesn't mean that you'll learn everything. And not studying doesn't mean that you'll remain in the dark forever. That's what makes things more difficult. You can't rest even for a moment, you're always tossing and turning. That's how life is—not just life, but everything in human history, generation after generation. It's exhausting. Exhausting to death. And …"

Kim Cheolsu listened in quiet.

"Of course it's different," I went on.

"What do you mean?"

"What you read was about *my* play."

"Oh, I was mistaken. I thought the play you wrote was based on the one written by Marx. So was it just the title that you borrowed?"

"Yeah."

"But …"

"But what?"

"It seems that someone would've mentioned the title somewhere, at least once, but I've never seen an article or anything

The Specters of Algeria

that said something about it. I mean, it *is* the only play that Marx ever wrote, even if it isn't well known. I guess it's never been published in Korea."

"No, it hasn't."

"But still."

"There's almost no one who's read it. And even less people know that it was written by Marx."

"Why is that? Because it's not a theoretical book? But wouldn't that have stirred up even greater interest? At least in Europe, though I can understand why that didn't happen in Korea."

"I know. But even in Europe, not that many people know that the work even exists. It went out of print a few years after it came out in Germany—it didn't sell very well, and rumor had it that it was forged. It was confirmed that Lily Müller did indeed work at the Hotel Victoria at the time Marx stayed in Algiers, but that doesn't prove that the work wasn't forged. Even Charles Longuet, who had seen Marx's letter, only remembered the play in parts, so there was no proving that the book was the same as what Marx had written."

"What about the French edition that Pak Seonwu got?"

"What about it?"

"Did it get a similar response in France?"

"Who knows?"

"Well, anyway, it doesn't seem likely that it was the only copy of the book. If it was, the owner of the bookshop wouldn't have just sold it. I mean, there's no way that he didn't know who Marx was."

"Maybe he thought it was a fake, too."

"What do you think?"

"About what?"

"Do you think it was fake?"

"Who knows?"

He took his eyes off me, and stayed still, looking deep in thought.

Getting up to put the table away, Yul said, "That's enough, Uncle Osu. You shouldn't tease an innocent young man like that."

"An innocent young man? He's over thirty."

Looking perplexed, Kim Cheolsu looked from me to Yul, and back again.

"Do you want the truth?" I asked.

Still looking perplexed, he nodded.

"The book that Pak Seonwu got wasn't the French edition."

"What was it, then?"

"It was the Korean edition published in North Korea."

"What?"

Pak Seonwu was a communist. He wanted to turn the Republic of Korea into a communist society. But he couldn't really picture it. He wanted to experience a communist society firsthand. He seriously considered defecting to North Korea. He thought for quite some time about what he would have to do in order to defect. Then he met someone who had similar ideas, someone he already knew, a guy named Pak Jaegi who was an upperclassman when they were in college. After graduation, Pak Jaegi joined a local broadcasting station, and was the head of a department there when they met again. He

The Specters of Algeria

shocked everyone by showing up at a reunion for the first time in ten years; then after everyone else left, he told Pak Seonwu something even more shocking.

"I'm defecting to North Korea," he said.

The words hadn't come out of nowhere. Pak Seonwu had stated that there was no hope for South Korea. In his youth, he had been ready to jump at any chance to act on his ideals, rudimentary as they were, to make a better society, but the words that came out of his mouth now were: "Nothing will make a difference."

Pak Seonwu had long grown accustomed to despair and lethargy, and after talking in this way he had asked, "Do you think North Korea is any different?"

"Sure it is," Pak Jaegi had replied.

Pak Jaegi had already met in secret with those from the North. The only reason why he was still in the South was because he had been instructed to get others who were of the same mind to join him before he defected; soon, he would be crossing the border.

And the reason why Pak Seonwu would later go to France was to receive an order. At Pak Jaegi's recommendation, he had become a trustworthy source for the North. When Pak Seonwu went to the place of rendezvous, the contact was reading a book: *The Specters of Algeria.* Talking about anything other than the order itself was forbidden, but Pak Seonwu detected something—someone following him, perhaps—and began to chat with the man as though he were an old friend; that was how they ended up talking about the book. As they chatted, Pak Seonwu began to take a genuine interest in the play, and touched by his enthusiasm, the man did his best to tell him all he knew about it. The book was deemed inferior to other works by Marx, he said, and only the chief government officials of North Korea had it in their possession, not making it available to the people; but he had been able to get a copy through his cousin, who had translated the book through an unofficial order, and found it much more interesting than what he had heard. When Pak Seonwu then showed an even keener interest, the contact gave it some thought, then gifted him the book.

"Just don't get caught. You'll get yourself into trouble, but I'll be severely punished as well," he said in his North Korean dialect.

Kim Cheolsu's eyes were wide open in astonishment.
"Then …"
"Then what?"
"Well … how do you know all these stories?"
Instead of answering him, I asked Yul to bring me another bottle of soju. She clicked her tongue but brought back a table set with plates of rolled omelet and kimchi along with the drink.
"Do you want the truth?" I asked Kim Cheolsu.
"Is there more … to the truth?"
"The truth is …"
He gave a gulp.
"I'm a spy, too," I said.
Kim Cheolsu stared fixedly at me, then turned his head to look at Yul. Yul was shaking her head from side to side. I let

out a guffaw. Kim Cheolsu stared at me for a long time, still looking dazed.

*

Pak Seonwu and his six friends were arrested in the summer of 1984, charged with forming an anti-government organization called "Chilhyeonhoe." Pegged as the ringleader, Pak Jaegi—Pak Seonwu's college friend—was rounded up along with them. He was charged with praising and aligning himself with the North Korean regime. It was revealed that Pak Jaegi and Pak Seonwu were responsible for contacting the North.

Three of the members in Chilhyeonhoe were teachers, and what they had said to students during class hours would serve as proof. *The arson that took place at the American Cultural Center in Busan was not initiated by communists; the polarization of wealth is the biggest structural problem in Korea; we must emulate the spirit of the April 19 Revolution.* The nature of Pak Seonwu's crime, in particular, was judged more serious because he had told his students not to believe everything the textbooks said and that they must face reality head on.

Chilhyeonhoe had also held memorial ceremonies for the May 18 Gwangju Massacre and studied banned books. They were mostly books written by defectors and antiestablishment authors from South Korea, along with some foreign books. *The Specters of Algeria* by Marx was one of them. This book was subject to greater suspicion because it was just a pile of general documents bound together, while the other books, whatever their nature, had at one time or another been published in South Korea. The prosecution decided that the banned books must have been copied and distributed by a resident spy.

Chilhyeonhoe and Pak Jaegi were taken into custody without a warrant and dragged to the basement of the anti-communist investigation office and subjected to all kinds of torture inflicted on them by an expert torturer. They were starved and kept from sleep for days, constantly assaulted in that state. They had to confess in detail as to how they had come to know one another and form the organization, what each of them had been in charge of, who else was involved, and what their future plans were. When their accounts differed, they were cast back to the torturer. Fifty or so days passed in this way.

4

"And?"

"And what?"

"What happened to them?"

"Four of them were sentenced to imprisonment, and the other four were put on probation."

"That was all?"

"About twenty years later, they were all acquitted in a new trial."

"All of them?"

"Do you find that strange?"

"No, but …"

"Is it Pak Seonwu and Pak Jaegi who trouble you?"

"Was it all a lie that they'd made contact with the North, and that they were communists?"

"What do you think?"

"Huh?"

"How much of it do you think is true, and how much of it not?"

"How would I …"

"You heard the whole story."

"But …"

"But what?"

"I haven't experienced it myself."

"Neither have I."

"So you've only heard the story, too?"

"Most of it."

"Are you saying that there's a missing part?"

"Yeah."

"What is it?"

"What do you think?"

Kim Cheolsu fell silent.

"Nothing you say will turn the truth into a lie, or vice versa. So just relax and spit it out."

"I … I don't know. I don't think it's something I can judge."

"Every story is a mixture of truth and lies. Even when people see and hear the same thing at the same place, they each recollect it differently. Sometimes, even what you hear and see and experience for yourself isn't true. You either experience it without realizing that it isn't true, or you just don't remember it correctly. Sometimes a lie turns into the truth, when someone believes it to be true. They could've been deceived, or they could've just believed it; they could've let themselves be deceived, or they could've *wanted* to be deceived. There's simply a number of different possibilities. It's something that you can't judge in the first place. So are you going to not judge, because it's something that can't be judged in the first place?"

Again, he fell into silence.

"But is it possible? To not judge?" I asked.

The Specters of Algeria

He remained silent.

"You're always judging. It's impossible not to judge when you're human. This is true, that is false. This is a lie that seems like the truth. That's a truth that seems like a lie. Now, say it."

"Say … what?"

"You listened to the story without doubting at times, but doubted and questioned and refuted things at other times, right?"

"That's right."

"That's what judging is."

He was quiet.

"So you'd be lying if you said that you can't judge."

He didn't say a word.

"But you're telling the truth when you say that you can't judge."

"Huh?"

"You can make judgments, but you can't judge whether or not something is true."

Silence.

"Then what can we do? About the things we see and hear and experience?" I asked.

"What *can* we do?"

"See, you're deferring to me again."

"I … I really don't understand. I don't understand at all what you're talking about."

"Then let me ask you again. How much of what I said do you think is true, and how much of it not?"

After some hesitation he said, "It all seems like the truth, but then it all seems like a lie."

"Do you even want to know what's true and what isn't?"

"Yes, I do."

"Then you should find out for yourself."

"But ... how?"

"Why are you asking me, my friend?"

Silence again.

"Do you even want to find out?"

"I think I do."

"You *think* you do. Do you want to, or not?"

More silence.

"If you can't answer that question, stop being curious and go on living your life the way you've been living it. And relax, because that doesn't mean that your life is meaningless."

"No, I don't want to."

"You mean, you can answer the question?"

"Yes."

"Then do it."

"I want to find out."

"How will you do that?"

"I will, somehow, in some way."

I heaved a deep sigh. He did the same.

"All right, good. You seem like a proper young man at last. That's wonderful. So I'll give you a hint."

Kim Cheolsu listened in silence.

"What you want to find out somehow, in some way. That. *That* is the truth."

Part Four

THE REMAINING STORY

I started getting drowsy after eating the in-flight meal. I pulled the blanket up to my neck and closed my eyes. I drifted in and out of sleep. The head of the person sitting next to me tilted in my direction, but luckily for me it didn't touch my shoulder. I lifted the window cover slightly, and bright light came pouring in. A passing stewardess asked in a whisper to please use the reading lamp, as many of the passengers were asleep. I lowered the window cover and turned on the lamp.

I pulled out *Germany. A Winter's Tale* from my bag. Kim Cheolsu had sent it to us recently. He sent two editions. One of them was the one Uncle Osu had lent him when he was in Jeju, and the other was a new edition published by a different company. He wrote in his letter that he had found, after comparing the two, that the previous edition had more mistranslations than he had assumed. The package he sent contained about a hundred pages of A4 printouts. It was a novel written by Yeonghee, he said. Yeonghee hadn't written a letter, but on the very first page was a short greeting in her handwriting.

How are you? I'm doing fine.

The title of the novel was *The Specters of Algeria.*

It took her more time to make up her mind to send you the novel than to write it. She was a bit embarrassed, I think, and a bit afraid as well. She actually wrote and discarded several letters. She gave up in the end, saying letters were more difficult to write than novels. If she knew I told you this, she'd be furious at me. She rarely gets angry but when she does, all hell breaks loose. She asked me to ask you if it would be all right for her to use the title, Kim Cheolsu said in his letter.

"Why even ask? It's not something I came up with in the first place," Uncle Osu said.

She also wanted to know if she could write a novel based on both your lives, and the lives of those around you, the letter went on to say.

"Well, she already did, didn't she?" was Uncle Osu's response.

And she asked that you tell her if some parts vary too much from the facts and bother you. I told her it would be fine, but she's quite worried, saying that you never know.

"What does she think I am?" Uncle Osu said.

"What do you mean?" I asked.

"If it's just facts, would it even be a novel?" he explained.

Kim Cheolsu was getting ready to put on a play. He wasn't directing it or writing it; he was to make an appearance as an actor. He would be playing the man who runs without ceasing in *A Hundred Years Ago Today.* He accepted the role only because it didn't have any lines—this would be the first and last time that he was onstage.

Germany. A Winter's Tale wasn't a book with many pages. It was my second time reading it, but I still had a hard time with it, and it ended up taking me two hours to finish. My eyes stung, so I turned off the lamp and closed them. I fell asleep before I knew it.

I had a dream. A woman was walking a tightrope. It was long and quite high up in the air. Her hair was very long and black. Whenever she jumped up and down on the rope, her hair scattered in all directions. She did a few somersaults and sprang high up into the air in the end. The red sun overlapped her face. At that moment, our eyes met. The woman smiled, baring her teeth. Then she landed straight onto the ground. She asked me my name. *Han Eunjo,* I said. *What's yours?* She replied, *Lily Müller.*

My body sank, and I woke up. The plane was rocking. An announcement came on, telling people to stay seated because of turbulence.

I cracked a smile, imagining what Uncle Osu would say if I told him I'd talked to Lily Müller in my dream. I turned on the reading lamp again. I had brought two more books besides the Heine. Both were mystery novels. Uncle Osu had recommended them to me, saying that there was nothing like a mystery novel to pass time on a boring flight. After trying to decide which one to read first, I put them both away and pulled out *The Specters of Algeria.* The book was a hardback, with a laminated cover; it looked quite decent, even on a second look. It had been custom ordered online. It was my idea to have the title printed in red against a black background. Uncle Osu made fun of me, saying I had no eye for design. *How did you spend twenty years altering clothes when you're that bad?* he said. I just ignored him.

The names of the authors were printed in white: Pak Hyeongmin, Jang Minseon, Han Jiseop, Baek Soi.

*

Uncle Osu said that he didn't know who came up with the title, either. "Probably your mom or Jing's dad," he said. "Or maybe it was your dad or Jing's mom." But he said that it was Jing's dad and my mom, for sure, who wrote the play. "But," he also said,

"I think the four of them came up with the story together, that's what I heard."

The four probably stayed up late into the night drinking and chatting as usual. At Jing's house. Or at mine. Someone probably started playing the guitar as they all got drunk. Someone probably sang, someone probably danced, and someone probably recited a poem. And they probably went on chatting.

Then someone probably said the line: "What on earth does it mean for someone to feel something about something?"

The words may have hovered in their mind for days, or they might have come in that moment like an inspiration; it could have been a passage they read somewhere, or an alteration of such a passage. The original words may have been something like, "What does it mean when someone feels something about something?"

Maybe it wasn't a line, but just a part of the chitchat.

The chitchat probably turned into a line, with the line calling for another line.

The Specters of Algeria

"Do you want to be human?"

Perhaps someone grumbled, saying that a question shouldn't be countered with a question. The dialogue probably continued in any case, as they went on saying one line after another. Or had they said the words hesitantly, one delayed line after another?

"Tell me a secret."

"A secret about what?"

"About anything."

Perhaps the title came first. One of them, perhaps, had actually been to a bar named Algeria. Perhaps someone had said that they wanted to go to the real Algeria.

I wonder who came up with the idea of Marx.

Uncle Osu told me that my dad asked him one day while having a drink together, "If Marx ever wrote a play, Osu, what do you think it would be about?"

Uncle Osu didn't remember what he said in reply. Probably something lame, he said, because he had a hard time imagining something like that at the time, just as he did now. He recalled my dad jumping on him, hearing his answer. *You never forget a humiliation like that,* he said.

It started out as a joke, my dad told him. But a story unfolded as they played around with it. My dad thought that was all, but my mom and Jing's dad said they wanted to write it up for real. So they decided to do a proper job of it, pull a big prank.

"What's significant about this play is Marx; that he wrote it," my dad had said.

"So, what—" Uncle Osu began to ask.

"I want to play a prank on the guys," my dad promptly replied.

"Huh?"

"Just imagine how they'll react when we tell them that it's the only play ever written by Marx. It'll be hilarious, don't you think?"

"You think … they'll fall for it?"

"Why not?"

"I mean, you play jokes on them all the time, so …"

"Well, that's because they're so out of it. Didn't they learn anything while growing up? They fall for every little thing I say."

"You said that's why you like them, because they're so good and innocent."

So their conversation continued, and Uncle Osu, in the end, decided to play accomplice in the fraud. He hadn't set out to do so, but as he persistently questioned my dad about the parts of the story that the other members of the troupe might doubt, and added details to his answers and helped fill the holes, the story became complete. Lily Müller took the longest. My dad raised objections about her story being too long, when she was only the messenger.

"A decent supporting role is what makes a work great," Uncle Osu said.

My dad whistled and said, "You have grown, my man!"

And finally, they came to Pak Seonwu. Uncle Osu said that it had to be an acquaintance of my dad who came upon the book in a used bookstore in Paris, and my dad immediately thought of Pak Seonwu. Uncle Osu didn't know who Pak Seonwu was.

"There's a book club held by Minseon. He's in it. He's a high school French teacher," my dad explained.

My dad would tell the other members of the troupe that the play was a work by Marx and hand out copies, they decided. *Oh, right. Marx. We've been fooled one too may times. What do you take us for?* they would say. With his face straight, my dad would tell them to give it a look, and Uncle Osu would start reading it, chuckling as he did. Then little by little, his face would harden. At the part where two of the characters gave each other names, Uncle Osu would say: "Fred? Fred is ... Engels's first name."

Then someone would be sure to ask, "It is?"

He would then say, "Yeah. Friedrich Engels. Whenever Marx wrote him a letter, he addressed him as Fred, short for Friedrich. And Hammonia ..."

"Who's that?"

"It's a name that appears in one of Heine's poems."

"Heine?"

"Don't tell me you don't know who Heine is. There's a part in one of his poems that goes, 'Who are you ... Where do you live, majestic dame? ... She smiled and said ... I am Hammonia, Hamburg's goddess protector!' Did you know that Heine and Marx were very close?"

Once the others were finished reading the play, Uncle Osu would ask my dad, "How on earth did you get a hold of this? Are we safe, with this in our possession?"

That would be the last line of the hoax. My dad and Uncle Osu howled with laughter, picturing the looks on the other members' faces.

"What do I do after that?"

"What is there to do? You just tell them that you're not sure, and tell them to decide for themselves what to do."

"What if I can't keep myself from cracking up?"

"You *have* to."

"And when do we tell them the truth?"

"I'm not sure ... but don't wait too long."

"How long is too long?"

"Don't let it go to the next day."

"Why not?"

"They could have trouble falling asleep."

Again, they chortled with laughter.

"All right, then. I'll hand out the plays before the rehearsal, and tell them the truth after we wrap up."

"Sounds good."

"I hope they have a good laugh over it, even if it's just for a day. Hopefully they'll smile whenever they think back on it."

The fraud did not succeed. Three days before my dad was to hand out the copies, my mom was arrested. So was Jing's dad. Five days after that, my dad and Jing's mom were arrested as well. I didn't see them being taken away. Uncle Osu took care of Jing and me. I don't remember if we stayed at my house, or at Jing's. I don't remember how long we stayed together like that, either.

Then one day.

Several men in black suits turned up at the house without warning. They stomped around the house, still in their shoes. Jing and I hid ourselves under a blanket as Uncle Osu instructed. Someone lifted the blanket, then let it fall. I began to cry, and Jing took my hand in his.

*

My mom and Jing's dad were members of Chilhyeon-hoe. *Chil* for seven, and *hyeon* for string: seven strings. Pak Seonwu had come up with the name, representing seven people strumming seven strings. Strumming strings stood for reading and reciting. The idea was to read each and every word in depth, as though they were strumming strings. The explanation gave meaning to the word, but the name came to him while he was reading *Chilhyeongeum*, the short story featuring a seven-stringed harp.

"And the lyre too, reach me the lyre, that I may sing a battle-song."

It was a line from a poem posted on the wall by the main character of the story. A poem by Heine. Pak Seonwu recited the line, then suggested that they name the book club "Chil-hyeonhoe." There were seven members in all, so everyone was pleased with it, saying it was just the thing.

The book club itself had been Pak Seonwu's idea. The members had belonged to the same club in college and had gotten together occasionally over drinks through the years.

When my mom and Jing's dad told us about the name, my dad snorted and said, "The guy's such a cornball."

"You've only met him a few times. How would you know?" my mom retorted.

"First of all, he's pretty, like a girl. He preens too much."

"When did he ever preen?"

"Why does he have to be so fancy with a name?"

"Oh, come on, you're just jealous."

"Jealous? Jealous, huh!"

"You try coming up with one, then."

"Come up with what?"

"A name for the book club."

"You're not even going to use it, though."

"We might, if it's better than Chilhyeonhoe."

My dad thought it over for a moment, then said, "UKKU."

"What's that?"

"It's the name of a ship."

"A ship, out of nowhere?"

"There's huge a ship that crosses the ocean. Hundreds of people can get on it. It says on the side, 'UKKU.'"

"So I'm asking you, what does it mean?"

"You and your meanings. Just picture the image. Fabulous, isn't it?"

"Unknowing the Known, Knowing the Unknown. You turn the unknown into the known, and the known into the unknown," Jing's mom said.

My dad was pleased. He said, "Oh, that's fantastic! Soi, you've always got the perfect clincher."

"Oh, you just love whatever Soi says, don't you?" my mom said.

"Jealous, are you?"

"Yeah, I'm jealous, you king of caprice!" my mom said.

Jing's mom broke into peals of laughter. So did Jing's dad, followed by my parents.

The Specters of Algeria

That was how the name UKKU came about, Jing's mom once told me. The day she told me that, she had had her memory back for quite a while. Then, fingering the letters "UKKU" on the cover of *The Specters of Algeria,* she said: *Where am I? And who are you?*

Chilhyeonhoe held two meetings a month. They alternated between discussions and readings. The members took turns selecting books to read. The ones they could buy at bookstores, they bought, and the ones they couldn't, the person who had chosen it made copies for the others. The copies were mostly of banned books. One of which had leaked by mistake and fell into the hands of the police, and so began the investigation.

It wasn't just my dad and Jing's mom who were investigated for being involved with Chilhyeonhoe. The families and acquaintances of Chilhyeonhoe members were all placed under interrogation. A little later, Uncle Osu and the members of his troupe were also taken away by the police, each at a different time. Their old college friends and even the people who had so much as heard of the book club were all taken away. Very few people, other than the old college friends, knew all the seven members of the club. Either they didn't know their names, or they had never seen them before.

The members of Chilhyeonhoe, other than my mom and Jing's dad, said that *The Specters of Algeria* was a work by Marx. Just as my dad and Uncle Osu were plotting a prank on the theater people, my mom and Jing's dad were planning on taking the book club members on a ride and had hinted that they had, with great difficulty, gotten a hold of the only play ever written by Marx in order to bait them.

The Specters of Algeria was found in Jing's house. There were thirty copies in all, and printed under the title on the first page were the words: *Written by Karl Marx*. The full account was given during the investigation, but the police didn't believe it. Or rather, they had no intention of believing it, Uncle Osu said.

"What was true or not didn't matter to them. Or I should say, the facts were predetermined. It wouldn't have made an ounce of difference if *The Specters of Algeria* had never existed in the first place."

*

"Won't you come with me?"

Jing had asked that day, stopping before getting into the taxi.

"Come with me," he had said, pulling me by my hand, but I didn't move. I did my best to stay still.

I looked back on the moment countless times. Why had I hesitated? What would have happened to us if Jing had asked me to come with him, not to the airport but somewhere far away, and I had gone with him? Where would we have gone? Would we have been happy throughout the years that passed?

"Why are you leaving? With me, and your mom, here?" I had asked him that day at the airport.

Had I really wanted to keep him from leaving? What would have happened to us if he hadn't left? Where would we have stayed? Would we have been happy throughout the years that passed?

Why had Jing left, and I stayed? Why had we decided to do that?

*

Several days after Jing's dad died, my dad went to see Jing. His mom wasn't home; she might have gone out for a walk, or to the hospital or the supermarket. Or maybe she was sleeping in her room. She slept whenever she could back then. She often slept all day, without opening her eyes once. On such days, Jing was afraid that his mom had died. He wanted to touch her to check on her, but fearing that she wouldn't move for real, he made an effort to look away, trying to believe that she was just sleeping. In any case, his mom is not a part of his memory of that day.

"I have something to tell you," my dad said, and fell into a long silence. Jing waited. He had some tea in the meantime. So did my dad. It was bay leaf tea. They always had bay leaf tea at Jing's house, made with leaves picked from our flowerbed. The tea was quite hot, so the two of them took very slow and little sips. Nothing more was said, even when they had emptied their cups.

"I'm sorry," my dad said at last.

Jing didn't know what to say.

"I'm sorry, Jing. I'm so sorry," my dad repeated.

Jing remained silent.

My dad put his cup to his lips, then put it back down, realizing it was empty. If there had been any tea left it would have spilt because his hands were shaking, Jing wrote.

It was a few summers ago that I got a letter from Jing. It had been sent to my old address in Seoul, and Yeonghee had sent it to me in Jeju. Jing was still in Finland, still working at that Korean restaurant. He was a better cook now, and the sous-chef there.

Jing boiled some water again and brewed more tea; again, the two of them drank very slowly. *And,* Jing said,

I thought I should accept his apology. I didn't need an apology, but it seemed that he wanted to apologize. So I decided to hear him out. For the last time. Yes, I think that somehow, I knew by then that I'd be leaving.

"Uncle Jiseop," he said, and my dad's hands began to tremble again.

"What are you so sorry about?" Jing asked.

My dad couldn't answer him right away.

"Uncle Jiseop," Jing called out again.

"We didn't know what we should do for one another. We'd spent so much time together, but we didn't know what to do for one another. We were all broken, and had to express that somehow to someone, anyone; but in the process, we damaged one another even further. When I thought on why we'd turned out the way we did, I couldn't bear it … I should've done something … but I … I didn't know what to do …"

His head hanging, my dad covered his eyes with his hand.

You may not believe me, Yul, but I'm on my way back. To you, and Mom. I've always thought that I should, though I

The Specters of Algeria

didn't know that it would take me so long, and I don't know how much longer it'll take. I wonder sometimes if I'm not just running away, rather than going back. You could say that, in a way, since I've waited for those days to grow distant from me. They will never be forgotten completely, but I hoped that they would grow distant, at least. Until the day when I'll be able to look back on them with indifference, as though looking at a painting on a wall. That's all I've done since those days.

Your dad told me that day before he left. That what he'd said before wasn't true. That he had just wanted to hurt someone, and I happened to be there. I guess he was referring to what he said about him and my mom sleeping together. But I already knew. His face had already told me as he blurted the words that day. The face had nothing to do with the words, the face I'd never seen before. I can't forget that look on his face. I just can't. I wondered, how long will that look stay on his face? How long will my mom keep herself locked up in her room? Wouldn't it be better somehow if they actually slept with each other? Wouldn't it be better, if they could love someone again? But would that have been possible for them?

My mom and I didn't leave together. I think she left soon after I did. My mom's memory had already begun to get mixed up by then, and I knew that I shouldn't leave her alone in that state.

I read an article on the Internet a few years ago saying that they had been exonerated. Did that put an end to it all? Maybe. But there's still so much that I don't know about them. How my dad and your mom came to start that book club, how it got caught up in something like that, what the other members were like, what they went through, who made them go through those things and why, what became of our parents' lives after what happened. And what became of your life. Is it too late to find it all out now? Or maybe I don't want to know to the end.

Should I have stayed, for better or worse? I did give the question some thought. So I came back, once. And I knew that I couldn't stay. I was afraid that all of it would become a part of me. That things I hadn't chosen would become a part of me, my memory, and in the end, my entire self. That look on your dad's face would become mine, and I would be the one locked up in my mom's room.

Yul. I knew that you wouldn't come with me. And that you wouldn't come here.

I'm sorry. I'm telling you at last.

I'm sorry. To you. And to my mom. To everyone I left behind.

I didn't write him back; I wasn't sure if I should tell him that his mom had already passed away. Time went by again, leaving me in this state of not knowing.

*

It's not that I know what to do now, and it's not that I've stopped thinking about what might have happened if Jing hadn't left, or if I had gone with him. I still try to imagine what things might have been like if nothing had happened. I still have a hard time imagining that. Still, I go on asking myself: *What should I have done? What should I do now?*

The Specters of Algeria

When I see you, will I tell you everything? Things you don't know but I do? When you see me, will you tell me everything? Things you know but I don't? About my days. Your days. And everyone's days. What will happen to the story neither you nor I know? Will it turn into a story that no one will ever know? Will it, then, be a story that never existed in the first place?

In a few hours I'll be seeing you. I can't imagine what we'll talk about, what we'll do, where we'll go. But we'll say something, do something, go somewhere. I'll be seeing you, still in the dark about everything, still not knowing what to do.

honfordstar.com